Praise for Jane Heller

"What's so great about Heller's writing is her wit."
—*Cleveland Plain-Dealer*

"Jane Heller is the literary master. She has an inimitable knack for crafting perfectly imperfect characters and dropping them into outrageous yet utterly believable situations where hilarity inevitably ensues. Heller's timing is flawless, her turns-of-phrase are peerless, and her endings never fail to satisfy. *Three Blonde Mice* is like the Dark Chocolate Marquise featured in the book (recipe included!): decadent, sexy, and over far too soon."
—Jenna McCarthy, author of *Everything's Relative*

"I loved *Three Blonde Mice*, a hilarious send-up of foodies and the farm-to-table movement. *Three Blonde Mice* is a delicious read—and there are no calories."
—Elaine Viets, author of *The Art of Murder: A Dead-End Job Mystery*

"I love Jane Heller's quirky off-kilter novels! In *Three Blonde Mice*, Heller and her keen-eyed wit cook up a wonderful satire on chic cooking classes, farm-to-table food groupie⸱⸱⸱ ⸱fs with the egos of rock stars. She dissects love-⸱⸱⸱ a murder plot—with the sharpness of ⸱⸱⸱ d every delicious moment."
—Melodi⸱ ⸱⸱y of Mirrors*

"If you've never tried a J⸱ ⸱⸱ook, you are missing out on some of the most del⸱ ⸱⸱ul, satirical and just plain fun books around."

—*RT Book Reviews*

Three Blonde Mice

JANE HELLER

DIVERSIONBOOKS

Also by Jane Heller

FICTION

Princess Charming   *Clean Sweep*

Best Enemies   *Sis Boom Bah*

Crystal Clear   *The Club*

Female Intelligence   *The Secret Ingredient*

Infernal Affairs   *An Ex to Grind*

Lucky Stars   *Some Nerve*

Name Dropping

NONFICTION

Confessions of a She-Fan

You'd Better Not Die or I'll Kill You

Diversion Books
A Division of Diversion Publishing Corp.
443 Park Avenue South, Suite 1008
New York, New York 10016
www.DiversionBooks.com

This is a work of fiction. Names, characters, places and incidents either are the product of the author's imagination or are used fictitiously. Any resemblance to actual persons, living or dead, events or locales is entirely coincidental.

For more information, email info@diversionbooks.com

First Diversion Books edition August 2015.
Print ISBN: 978-1-68230-285-9
eBook ISBN: 978-1-68230-284-2

For Elaine, Jackie, and Pat, my farm fatales,
whose friendship inspired me to bring them back.

Prologue

The fingers hovered over the laptop's keyboard, fidgeting and flexing, poised to begin typing. And then suddenly, propelled by the writer's burst of inspiration or clarity of purpose, they were off, racing over the keys in a manic hurry. Within minutes, the following words appeared on the screen:

Dear Pudding,

Did you know I call you Pudding, by the way? No, of course not. The name came to me as I was watching your cooking video on YouTube. You were talking about how you've loved pudding since you were a kid—chocolate pudding, banana pudding, rice pudding, tapioca pudding, sticky date pudding with caramel sauce. I had this hilarious image of your body dissolving into a vat of thick, spongy, gelatinous pudding, sort of like the Killer Robot from Terminator 2 *melting into liquid metal or the Stay Puft Marshmallow Man in* Ghostbusters *transforming into the gummy white goop that buries Manhattan. Listen to* me carry on about movie villains. Too much time on my hands, I guess.

Anyway, I signed up to be a guest at the hotel's Cultivate Our Bounty week just so I could get close to you, but since we won't have quality time alone until the very end, I thought I should write a quick note to say how much I despise you.

Yes, despise you. Does it scare you to hear that? Are you shocked that someone doesn't think you're God's greatest gift to the world? I'll pretend to be your fan for the entire week, and you'll probably buy my act, because you don't have a clue. You walk around like you're this important chef, someone whose passion in the kitchen we're supposed to admire, but we both know you're in it for the money and the ego. You're all about having foodies slobber over you as a promoter of the farm-to-table movement—excuse me, the farm-to-fork movement. Or is it plough-to-plate, cow-to-kitchen, barn-to-bistro, or mulch-to-meal? I can't keep track of your terminology anymore, can you? Bottom line: There's only one movement you promote, and it's your own.

You're a fraud—100 percent con artist. You wouldn't know authenticity if it hit you over the head with one of your overpriced cast iron skillets. You have the image of this do-gooder who's all about the land and the farmer and the planet, when in fact you have no conscience, no remorse for your actions. Do you know how much those actions enrage me? Enrage me, as in pure, unprocessed, non-genetically modified rage. If you don't get that, you will—as soon as it sinks in that your miserable life is nearly over. When that happens, your instinct will be to use this letter to protect yourself, but you won't show it to anybody—not the police, not even the little toads who work for you, because you have *too many secrets of your own and can't risk the exposure. Pretty interesting predicament you're in, wouldn't you say?*

I'm sorry about having to kill you on Saturday at the Bounty Fest thing. Not because you deserve to live—we're all better off with you dead, believe me—but because killing isn't something I do on a regular basis, and I really don't want to get caught. There's always the chance that some unlucky bastards could show up in the wrong place at the wrong time, and I'd have to take them out too. Still, while I'd rather not commit multiple murders, killing you will be so satisfying after what you did that I'll just have to shrug off potential collateral damage. Besides, any idiots who fall for your Cultivate Our Bounty bullshit deserve whatever they get.

The fingers sagged over the keys, depleted after their flurry of activity, but eventually directed the cursor to the navigation bar, clicked "file," then "print." Seconds later, the Dear Pudding missive materialized on plain white paper, ready to be sent to its recipient or, perhaps, delivered in person.

Day One:
Monday, July 15

1

"Welcome. Welcome," said the woman who was standing in the center of the room. Fifty-something years old, she had a weathered but pleasant-looking face and wore a Whitley-logoed T-shirt with a pair of blue jeans. Her gray hair was fashioned into two long, age-inappropriate braids. If she'd had a beard and mustache, she would have been the spitting image of Willie Nelson. "I'm Rebecca Kissel, Whitley's executive director. I'm so pleased that you've chosen us for your agritourism experience and are here at our Welcome Happy Hour. We've got an exciting week planned for you, and the weather is supposed to cooperate, so I know it'll be fun as well as educational. You'll enjoy meeting our in-house staff as well as your fellow agritourists, but the highlight will be your interactions with the renowned farm-to-table master we've snagged for you: Chef Jason Hill, who personifies clean, sustainable food that's as beautiful to look at as it is to eat. He'll be your instructor this week as our artisan in residence and will preside over our Saturday Bounty Fest finale to which we invite our non-Cultivate-Our-Bounty guests as well as members of the community."

She nodded at a long table set up across Whitley's Harvest Room, a serene space that overlooked infinite pastures. It was painted in the palest yellow and decorated in a neutral palette of bleached oak flooring and oversized white slipcovered chairs. There were also strategically placed white poufs—cubes that doubled as ottomans on top of which rested reading materials about the property's rich agricultural history.

"Before you leave tonight," she continued, "please stop by the hospitality table and pick up your personal earth-friendly, 100 percent recycled cotton Whitley tote bag. There's one for each of our agritourists as well as one for Chef Hill—you'll see your name tag pinned to your bag— and it contains maps of the property, a biography of Chef Hill, his recipes that you'll be preparing, a copy of his latest cookbook, the schedule of events, and lots more. The tote bags are handy because you can repurpose them for the beach, for work, for groceries, for gardening, whatever you like." She beamed, as if she were about to announce a cure for cancer. "You'll really appreciate the bags after you've cooked with us this week. Just think how much fun it'll be to bring your homemade fruit preserves, pickled vegetables, and raw nut balls to your friends and neighbors!"

"Speaking of nut balls, whose idea was this trip anyway?" I said to my best pals, Jackie Gault and Pat Kovecky, as we huddled together in a room full of strangers at the start of our week's vacation. Well, more precisely it was a "haycation" because we were staying on a farm.

No, we weren't camping out in some broken-down

barn. Please. I'm a person who has standing appointments for twice-weekly blowouts. We'd booked the Cultivate Our Bounty package at Whitley Farm, a Relais & Chateaux resort in Litchfield, Connecticut. It boasted a restaurant headed by a James Beard Award nominee and guest cottages outfitted with four-poster king-size beds swathed in Frette linens and layers of down, and we were there to learn where our food comes from and take culinary classes so we'd be able to cook the stuff. We would be milking a cow and making cheese from that milk; selecting a grass-fed, pasture-raised chicken and then roasting it with herbs we picked in the garden; foraging among the weeds for elderberries, milkweed, and other oddities of nature and then turning them into edible menu items. From Whitley's brochure: "Our goal is to increase understanding and appreciation of the land and the food it provides by giving our agritourists the opportunity to cultivate the bounty that sustains us while experiencing true farm-to-table cooking."

"It was my idea," said Jackie in her low, husky voice. "I thought the Three Blonde Mice deserved a week that didn't involve a hit man and a wacko ex-husband." She knocked back the last of her wine and heaved a grateful sigh, as if she'd been waiting all day for that glass. She preferred hardcore alcohol like bourbon and Scotch but would drink anything you put in front of her—too much of it lately, if you asked me. As for her "Three Blonde Mice" bit, it was the nursery rhyme nickname I'd given the three of us when we met seven years ago, and not because we were mousy. My hair was shoulder length and highlighted to a near platinum blonde; Jackie's was cut short and utilitarian like a punk boy's, spiky and strawberry; Pat's was a maze of tight frizzy curls—the color of oatmeal with glints of gray.

"I think it'll be enlightening," said Pat, after a decorous sip of her wine. She held her glass with her pinky extended like someone drinking tea out of one of those itsy bitsy china cups. "A nice change from last year's trip, that's for sure."

"I'm counting on it," said Jackie.

We took vacations together every year, and the last one was a disaster: a seven-day cruise to the Caribbean on an enormous floating hotel called the *Princess Charming*, during which Jackie's ex-husband Peter had hired one of the other passengers to kill her on the ship. Yes, kill her. (The would-be hit man was in the dining room with us every night. At the 6:30 early-bird seating, if you can believe it.) On top of that, she and Peter had been partners in J&P Nursery, a landscaping and gardening center in Bedford, a New York suburb frequently referred to as one of the most posh hamlets in America. The nursery serviced the fifty-acre estates of Wall Street hedge fund managers who viewed themselves as country gentlemen and therefore bought a lot of topiary. But when Peter turned out to be a crook, a cad, and a creep, and was carted off to the big house, the business became Jackie's responsibility.

Pat gave Jackie's arm an affectionate squeeze. "We won't let anything or anyone upset the apple tart this week, don't you worry."

"Apple *cart*, Pat." I always tried to restrain myself from correcting her, but, despite her privileged upbringing and Ivy League education, she was hopelessly susceptible to malapropisms and often spoke in sentences you'd expect to hear from a foreign exchange student. "I'm sure apple tarts will figure into our week here though."

I polished off my glass of Whitley Farm's Merlot-Petit Sirah. It was pretty decent for a blend produced in Connecticut, which was not, after all, California. In California, we'd be blathering about how a wine's structure, balance, and aroma were a religious experience. Not that I was a wine connoisseur. I drank red mostly because it was packed with life-saving antioxidants, allegedly. Women my age—I'm on the diminished-estrogen-level side of forty-five and a borderline hypochondriac—need all the help we can get.

"Now that you're all sufficiently lubricated, are you ready for our Whitley Mystery Challenge?" asked Rebecca, our fearless leader, as servers clad in yellow aprons that matched the walls stood at attention over by the table where our tote bags awaited us.

"Mystery Challenge?" I rolled my eyes. "I hate mysteries. They're in the same category as surprises, and you know how I feel about those."

"*Elaine*," Jackie groaned. "Try to just go with the flow for a change."

"Your servers are going to blindfold you," Rebecca explained, "and then you'll taste several of Chef Hill's offerings that showcase Whitley's commitment to sustainable food systems. You'll smell and touch each bite, savor it, and explore the culinary experience. Afterwards, you'll remove your blindfolds, and we'll discuss what you were eating, and you can assess your palate's ability to identify flavor profiles. This is how you'll begin to cultivate your bounty and learn where it comes from."

"Give me a break. Do we really need to know where our *bounty* comes from?" I said. "Personally, I think people who obsess about whether their salmon is sockeye or chinook are schnooks. It's a piece of fish, not a priceless diamond, and all it does is swim through my intestinal tract and land in my toilet bowl. And foraging? Seriously? What if we get Lyme disease from traipsing through the woods, not to mention poison ivy? Oh, and *The Huffington Post* had an article the other day about a man who drank raw milk from a farm like Whitley and came down with Guillain-Barré syndrome."

"*Elaine.*" Jackie groaned again, while Pat giggled.

Okay, I admit I was risk-averse and paranoid, anticipating danger, disaster, and death when no possibility of these things existed. Such traits could be amusing if you were a friend and irritating if you weren't.

"You'll end up liking this trip," said Jackie, as a rosy-cheeked male server with a mullet headed our way carrying something that wasn't food. "You're just being your usual neurotic self."

She was probably right. She and Pat knew me better than almost anyone. We'd met at a New York courthouse the day we'd all shown up to divorce our worthless spouses. Twenty minutes after our chance encounter in that musty, charmless lobby, we'd moved from consoling each other about our exes to celebrating our shared courage in shedding them, and then we'd ditched our lawyers and gone out for lunch—a long lunch involving a piano player who sang "Hey Jude" and kept extorting everybody to join in, which nobody did. Many more get-togethers followed, and the Three Blonde Mice became as close as sisters. It didn't matter that we were very different in terms of personality and background. We genuinely cared about the friendship, and nurtured it.

"And while you may not want to learn all this farm stuff, I do," Jackie went on. "A lot of my customers are installing vegetable and herb gardens on their properties, and I need to be knowledgeable about it. Besides, Chef Hill is kind of hot from what I've seen of him on TV." She wiggled her hips. "Maybe I'll get lucky."

Ever since Peter had traded my tomboy, whiskey-voiced friend for a simpering girly girl named Trish who probably wore her pearls to bed, Jackie had been on the prowl for men who would validate her sex appeal, and her quest only intensified after their divorce. She talked incessantly about getting laid or wishing she could.

"And I'll learn how to cook healthier meals for Bill and the children," said Pat.

Pat's husband was a gastroenterologist named Bill or, as I'd dubbed him, the God of Gastroenterology. He was a celebrity doctor, the guardian of the country's collective digestive system, and he popped up on *Good Morning America* whenever there was a national outbreak of E. coli. After a few years of letting his big, know-it-all personality overshadow her gentle, supportive one, Pat had decided enough was enough and divorced him. Eventually, he realized what a dope he'd been—it's not every day you find a woman of Pat's devotion and utter goodness—and came crawling back. They re-married, to the delight of their five teenagers—four boys, and a girl who had Pat's squat, pear-shaped body and round, full face along with her sweet nature and shining blue eyes.

"I get that you both have your agendas for this week,"

I said, "but being educated about the lifespan of a zucchini blossom isn't my idea of a good time."

Our server arrived, interrupting our back-and-forth. "Good evening. I'm Oliver, and I'll be working with you for the Mystery Challenge." He held up three black eye masks of the type used for either a good night's sleep or a date with the guy from *Fifty Shades of Grey*, and slipped a blindfold over our eyes. "Now I'll fetch your challenge items. Be back in a few."

Suddenly, I was in total darkness, and I did not enjoy the feeling. Nor did I appreciate having my eye makeup smudged.

"It's Oliver again," said our server after we had stood silently for a few minutes, awaiting his return. It was as if losing our sight had infantilized us, rendering us mute as well as blind. "I've got a tray of food here—three different bites for each of you ladies. I'll guide your hands to the bites and you can sample them. After your blindfolds come off, you'll tell Rebecca what you ate. Ready?"

"Yup, me first, Ollie," said Jackie. "I'm starving."

"Okay, I'm picking up your right hand now and directing it to one of the bites," he said.

"Hm. Slippery," said Jackie. "The hors d'oeuvre, not you, Ollie."

"Take your time with it," he said. "Really savor it."

I could hear Jackie chewing. She was a loud chewer even when she wasn't *savoring.* "Very tasty," she said. "I could wolf down a dozen more of these, whatever they are."

"I'll go next," chirped Pat.

While my friends were playing Whitley's little mystery game with Oliver, I lifted my blindfold just enough to sneak a peek at the tray of Chef Hill's tidbits. Call me a cheater if you must, but I wasn't about to eat just anything. My blood pressure was ninety over seventy for good reason. My cholesterol level was an impressive 160. And I weighed 130 pounds, which, for a middle-aged woman of my nearly six-foot height, made me a giantess with a model's figure—if not the staggeringly beautiful face. Why was I such a healthy specimen? Because I was in control at all times. I mean what if something on that tray was a cow testicle or an octopus heart, one of those "chef's specialty" items you see on restaurant menus nowadays, and I spent the rest of the week with my head over the porcelain throne?

Whew. Jackie's slippery thing is just a deviled egg, I thought with relief when I had my 20/20 vision back. It didn't look like the mayonnaise-and-mustard-with-paprika kind my mother used to make for company, but an egg was an egg. The second item was a piece of fruit—a peach maybe— with a dollop of cheese and some sort of herb or other. And mystery bite number three was meat—chicken, probably— sandwiched between two potato—

"Your turn, Elaine," said Pat, interrupting my stealth mission.

I fake coughed, covering my mouth with both hands so no one would notice that I was reaching up and surreptitiously sliding the blindfold down over my eyes. And then I made a performance out of letting Oliver help me navigate the bites into my mouth, smacking my lips ostentatiously and emitting "ah" and "hmm" noises as if I gave a shit what I was eating and whether it was grown at Whitley or bought at the nearest Stop & Shop. "Wow, that was intense," I said when I was done.

Oliver gave us permission to remove our blindfolds and thanked us for our participation.

"Now comes the test," said Rebecca once all the guests had finished the exercise. She was still in the center of the room but was now holding a clipboard and pen. "Let's find out who was able to identify the bounty. Anybody?"

My hand shot up. Why not have a little fun with these people, I figured.

"Yes," said Rebecca, nodding at me. "The woman in the beige sweater. Your name?"

Obviously she had no fashion sense, as my sweater was not *beige*. It was lightweight summer cashmere I'd gotten at last year's Labor Day sale at Bloomie's and its color was oatmeal. "Elaine Zimmerman," I said. "I believe I ate an egg stuffed with beets, apples, and blue cheese, a wine-soaked peach with a smear of herbed goat cheese and a sprig of mint, and braised chicken served between potato crisps and topped with a lemon aioli." I smiled and waited to be told that I had just aced the class, the week, the trip.

"You fucking peeked," Jackie hissed. She pretended to look mad, but she was laughing. "You're such a fucking baby."

"I am not," I hissed back. Jackie loved using the f-word in all its iterations. She was so earthy. "I was only 'going with the flow' like you wanted me to."

"Not now," Pat scolded. "You two can hatch this out later."

"There's nothing to *hash* out," I said, compelled yet again to correct her.

"I appreciate your contribution, Elaine," said Rebecca, scribbling my answers on her clipboard as the other guests murmured among themselves, no doubt astonished to have such a gastronome in their midst. "I think you'll benefit greatly from your week here."

"See that?" I whispered to my friends. "Willie Nelson thinks I'm good at cultivating my bounty."

"Unfortunately, you didn't identify any of the foods correctly except the hard-boiled egg," said Rebecca, sending me into a state of sheer mortification. "And before I let the others give us their answers, let me boast about our eggs here at Whitley. They're a product of our Rhode Island Red laying hens, which are fed our organic, certified soy-free meals so they'll lay beautiful big brown eggs. During the summer, when there's lots of sunlight, they lay about six per week per hen."

"Fascinating," I muttered. "Just riveting."

I sulked while the other guests threw out their answers. I went into a complete snit when one of them, a young woman who looked like a walking juice cleanse, got every ingredient right.

"Don't feel bad," said Jackie, slinging an arm around my waist and squelching another laugh. "So the egg was stuffed with radishes, not beets. They're both red."

"And your peach turned out to be a pear, but they both start with *p*," said Pat, with a not-very-straight face.

"You couldn't even cheat your way through," Jackie said. She and Pat could no longer contain themselves and were now doubled over, cackling.

I was about to point out that my friends didn't try to guess what the mystery foods were when an extremely attractive man tapped me on the shoulder.

"Sorry to intrude, but I just wanted to say that I admire your courage for being the first to raise your hand," he said as I took a quick inventory of his refined, almost patrician appearance. Those soulful brown eyes! That lustrous brown hair curling under his ears! That Cartier tank watch that cost way more than the knockoff I'd bought off a street vendor! The rest of his wardrobe wasn't cheap either; his shirt, slacks, and loafers were straight out of an Armani ad. And—most appealing of all—there was no wedding ring. "Your braised chicken idea wasn't that far off the mark. Quail can be hard to identify."

"Thanks," I said. "I appreciate that." He had a jovial air about him, a good-natured, nonjudgmental demeanor. "I'm Elaine Zimmerman, and these are my friends Jackie Gault and Pat Kovecky."

"Jonathan Birnbaum," he said during our round of handshakes. "Nice to meet you all."

"Do you work at Whitley or are you an agritourist like us?" asked Jackie.

"The latter," said this Jonathan Birnbaum person, who, although Jackie had posed the question, continued to concentrate on me, which was both unnerving and flattering. "I came primarily for the cooking classes. How about you, Elaine? What brought you to Whitley?"

"The bounty," I said without missing a beat. "Cultivating it, I mean. I have so much to learn, as you can tell from the Mystery Challenge. And I'm looking forward to the cooking, of course."

"Perfect," he said with a gleam in those brown eyes. "We'll be in the trenches together all week, Elaine."

Suddenly, things were looking up. Maybe Jonathan Birnbaum and I would embark on a torrid affair during Cultivate Our Bounty week. Maybe that affair would evolve into a meaningful relationship, one with stimulating conversations and stimulating sex and safety deposit boxes stuffed with Cartier jewelry. Maybe being dragged to Whitley was the best thing that would ever happen to me.

Of course, there was a slight complication. I already had a boyfriend.

2

"Home sweet home," I said out loud upon entering my cottage. After depositing the tote bag of Whitley handouts in the corner near my emptied luggage, I sank into the armchair to the right of the king-size four-poster bed. Other amenities of my accommodations included a marble bathroom with a soaking tub and rainfall shower, a desk area that offered Wi-Fi, an iPod dock and a fifty-inch flat-screen TV—pretty swanky for a farm.

I was tired and therefore grateful for the early night, particularly since we'd be forced to get up at the crack of dawn the next morning to shovel cow dung or something. Still, the evening had ended on a high note. Jonathan Birnbaum and I had chatted for a few more minutes while Jackie scurried off to the bar and Pat scurried off to the restroom. (Before departing, Jackie had mouthed, "He's hot," the same thing she said about most men, although in this case she was spot-on.) Jonathan told me he was a partner at his late father's law firm in Palm Beach, specializing in estates, wills and trusts; I told him I was a VP and senior account executive at Pearson & Strulley, the international PR firm where I'd worked for nine years. He told me he lived in a Mediterranean-style house with a pool and a tennis court across the street from the Intracoastal Waterway; I told him I lived in a two-bedroom, two-bath apartment in a doorman building on Manhattan's Upper East Side across the street from Madonna. He told me he was an accomplished home cook. I told him I was an accomplished orderer from restaurants that delivered, which made him laugh, which made me laugh, and before I knew it we were chuckling like fools. He said he wasn't expecting to "click with anyone" at Whitley and he was looking forward to the week. I said, "Me too," and then we said goodnight. He was definitely hitting on me, my friends confirmed later, and I have to say I didn't hate it.

I heaved a contented sigh, reached into the pocket of my white linen pants, and pulled out my cellphone to turn it back on since electronic devices were a no-no while the week's activities were in progress. I had no desire to post selfies or food porn on my Instagram page, but it was torture for me not to be able to get e-mails and texts. I liked to feel needed.

I checked the phone. Nothing. Bah.

I was about to connect it to its charger and put it and myself to bed when it rang.

My heart did a little dance when I saw that the caller was Simon, the boyfriend I mentioned. He and I had broken up shortly before the trip, so he was not, technically, my boyfriend, but that didn't stop my pulse from quickening every time I heard his damn voice,

"What?" I said in a not-very-cordial greeting.

"Hey, Slim. How's it going in Farmaggedon?" said Simon, clearly trying to be charming in that way he had of turning everything into a joke. "Were you out tilling the soil or picking berries for that pie you'll be baking for me?"

"I was at a party," I said, determined to sound chilly yet irresistible, like a heroine from a classic movie, say Lauren Bacall.

"Look, I know you hate me right now, but I love you and I'll prove it," he said. "You'll see."

"I won't hold my breath." How dare he try to reel me back in? We were done. I'd ended it. And, trust me, it hadn't been easy.

"Don't you remember how good it was between us, Slim?"

Of course I remembered. That was the problem. I'd met Simon Purdys on the *Princess Charming* and, after a lifetime of mistrusting men, I'd allowed myself to trust Simon. We'd entered into a passionate romance after our shipboard fling, a serious, sappy romance of the type where you can't bear to be without the other person for more than an hour and even an hour is a stretch. For a year it was miraculous and unexpected and beyond my wildest dreams, but not anymore. "What's the point of this call, Simon?"

"To cheer you up," he said. "You seemed pretty miserable the last time I saw you."

"Yeah, because I was angry. People aren't jumping for joy when they're ending a relationship."

I had shared the details of the breakup with Jackie and Pat, of course, and they both thought it was my fault. Some friends.

"Don't be a fucking idiot. He's a keeper," Jackie had said.

"I wouldn't give him up if I were you," Pat had advised. "He's a special, special man, Elaine."

He'd certainly seemed to be. He'd been a well-regarded travel writer at *Away from It All* magazine when we met on the ship. He'd been thinking of resigning; he'd said he was tired of traveling so much. Then shortly after we got back from the cruise, his publisher offered him the editor-in-chief position, and he grabbed it, thinking a desk job would mean less time on a plane and more time for a life. Wrong. He was in nonstop meetings, buried under an executive's workload. I could handle that, no problem, since I was a workaholic myself.

But then he hired—no, campaigned for—Mallory Ryan to join the team as editorial director of afia.com, the magazine's website. Like every other magazine, *Away from It All* had experienced flagging newsstand and subscription sales and needed its digital operations to pull in more eyeballs. Since Mallory was a tech genius with a reputation for efficiently bringing print media into the twenty-first century, and she was ambitious, stupidly gorgeous, and only twenty-eight years old (the horror), Simon had convinced his boss to open his corporate wallet for her. I wasn't thrilled that my boyfriend spent many hours of the day and night canoodling with her about memes and gigabytes and platforms, nor was I wild about hearing Mallory this and Mallory that whenever we were together. (He wasn't wild about my nicknames for Mallory either: "the Web Wench" for obvious reasons and "Mammary" due to her big gazongas.) I'm sure she was a delightful person, but the fact was this: He claimed to love me but hadn't asked me to marry him or live with him or even leave a toothbrush at his apartment. Not in the year that we'd been together. Had she bumped me out of contention?

Or was he simply a commitmentphobe? He would tell me—I'm saying he himself would speak the words without any provocation from or prompting by me—that he wanted the same sort of coupledom that I did, but then he would go through periods when he would avoid the subject as if it had crab lice. It was a pattern, and it drove me nuts. He would get me all hopeful and excited about our future and then drop me on my ass if I tried to pin him down on the specifics, and I'd had it up to here with his flip-flopping.

"Well, we don't have to get into things tonight," said Simon. "I just wanted to wish you luck with all the farming." He laughed. "Still trying to picture you as that pioneer woman on the Food Network. What's her name?"

"Ree Drummond, and she lives on a ranch, not a farm. She's married to a cowboy." I'm sorry to tell you that I emphasized the word "married" because I couldn't help sticking it to him that he and I weren't.

"I meant that I know you're out of your element up there," he said, his tone softening. "I hope you'll meet some nice people. Really, Slim."

"As a matter of fact, I already did," I said with a gleeful lilt in my voice, "and he's extremely nice."

"He?"

"Goodnight, Simon."

Day Two:
Tuesday, July 16

3

"The land is divided into twelve plots, and we grow around 200 varieties of vegetables," enthused Rebecca, the Willie Nelson look-alike. My friends and I and the seven other members of our group stood beside a row of red and golden beets. "Behind us is celeriac, chard, and kale, and down below we have cabbage and corn. At the top of the hill we have hops that are used by craft breweries in the area...."

Blah blah blah. It was 9:00 a.m. and the day was a scorcher already—not a hint of a breeze, not a single cloud in the sky. Just hot, muggy air that made my hair frizz, my body clammy, and my brain yearn for my meat-locker-cold office where flies didn't dive-bomb my neck and the sun's rays didn't bore through my broad-spectrum SPF 100 moisturizer. I wondered how I would survive the week.

Don't get me wrong. Whitley Farm was breathtaking—the stuff of landscape painters—but harvesting my own kohlrabi wasn't high on my bucket list. I was more interested in getting into the presumably air conditioned kitchen.

"We also do a lot of inter-cropping, so we plant green manures in between actual food crops…."

More blah blah blah. I tried to look nonchalant as I scanned the group for Jonathan, and he gave me a big smile when our eyes met. *Yes, he'll be the bright spot*, I thought, as Rebecca asked us to introduce ourselves and explain what had brought us to Whitley's Cultivate Our Bounty week.

"We have one more agritourist coming," she added. "He'll be joining us in the kitchen after our foraging expedition. In the meantime, let's have those of you who are here get to know one another, shall we?"

"At least the person coming later is a man," Jackie whispered before the introductions. "There aren't many in this group, and Elaine has already staked out the hot guy, so having one more gives me a fighting chance at some action."

"I asked Bill to fix you up with that doctor," said Pat, "but you didn't like him."

"The proctologist?" Jackie shuddered. "All he wanted to do was stick his finger where it doesn't belong."

"If the ladies over there are finished, I'll go first. I'm Lake Vanderkloot-Arnold," said a thirty-something who would have been pretty except that she didn't look human. What I mean is she had the figure of a lollipop—all head and no body. I was thin for my giantess height, but she was as skinny as a haricot vert, with only the occasional ripple of muscle in her arms and legs. Her long dark hair was pulled back into a perky ponytail and she was dressed in Lululemon yoga wear. She bounced on the balls of her feet when she spoke, which suggested abundant energy and vivacity, but her face was drawn, her skin sandpaper dry, and her collarbones protruded from her pale blue tank top. In the daylight, I realized she was the one who'd guessed all the right answers to last night's Mystery Challenge. "My life partner and I live in Manhattan—I volunteer at the Guggenheim, and he's in commercial real estate at Cushman & Wakefield—and we came to Whitley because we're true believers in the farm-to-table movement. We shun restaurants that don't use the freshest, locally sourced ingredients and we bring our own food to dinner parties if we think the host is serving anything processed. We've been yearning to take our journey deeper by honing our cooking skills to reflect and honor the land. If you don't honor the land and its bounty, you can't really walk the walk."

Okay, who in their right mind talked like that? And what cooking skills was she referring to? Her idea of a meal was probably a chia seed.

"I'm Lake's husband Gabriel," said the man she had called her life partner. He was as body-perfect as she was body-deprived, attractive in a slightly hawkish, predatory way. He had a long, angular face with a sharp nose and chin, and he wore his brown hair in a man bun, which, given that he worked in the corporate world, he probably trotted out only during his downtime. His heather-green cargo shorts and stretchy yellow shirt revealed taut, professional-athlete-grade thighs and abs that were so perfectly sculpted they looked like implants. "As Lake said, we take care of ourselves, and that means being vigilant about what we eat. I can promise you that nothing goes into *this* mouth unless I know where it comes from." He pointed emphatically to his mouth in case we mistook it for his ear or eye.

I kept waiting for the Vanderkloot-Arnolds to laugh or make a snarky remark to show us they had a sense of irony or were just plain joking, but no. Again I had the thought that it would be a long week.

"I'm Connie Gumpers," said a woman who gave us all a little wave. She was in her late fifties, short and chunky, with a muffin top she didn't try to camouflage with a tunic like many middle-aged women in Manhattan. Instead she wore a too-tight Green Bay Packers T-shirt with her blue jeans and sneakers. There was something equally refreshing and low maintenance about her brassy blonde hair with visible gray roots, which hung at random around her ears. "My husband Ronnie and I live in Kenosha, Wisconsin. Our grandkids were begging us to take a cooking trip for our anniversary because they know their Gammy watches food shows 24/7."

"She sure does," said Ronnie, a heavyset man whose jeans strained to contain his bulk, and whose balding head carried the burden of three chins. He was sweating profusely, and I feared he might collapse in the heat. "Bobby Flay's her favorite TV chef, but she also goes crazy for that judge on *Chopped*." He turned to his wife. "What's his name, Cupcake? The one with the tan and the fancy suits?"

"Geoffrey Zakarian," she said. "He's a dreamboat. But I love the whole bunch of them—Giada, Ina, Rachael, Guy, and especially Jason Hill. I've followed him to other cooking demonstrations and now I'll be seeing him again this week. Yay!"

"She's a hoot, isn't she?" Ronnie nodded at his wife affectionately. "Wonderful, wonderful mom and grandma. All those years I was building my building business? She took care of everything at home, kept it all running like clockwork. Now I'm retired, and we're living the high life." He paused to catch his breath. He was sort of wheezing.

"She does her chef thing, and I let her drag me along for the ride. I say 'drag me along' because I'm not all that gung-ho on the healthy this, healthy that. Give me a four-cheese Whopper with a side of onion rings and I'm a happy man." He chuckled. "I love to eat—so does Cupcake—but we do other fun things together too. We learned how to restore old clocks, took a course in woodworking, went with the grandkids to Comic Con, the convention where all the superhero actors go to plug their movies. And we spent a couple of weeks in Gay Paree." He chuckled again, guiltily this time. "I guess I'm not supposed to say that anymore. Sorry if I offended anybody. Great people, the gays. The French too. They get a bad rap for being uppity, but they were friendly as all get out when we were over there. Now here we are doing the Cultivate Our Bounty thing with you nice folks because Connie wanted to see her chef and we're celebrating our anniversary. Good, good times."

I gave Jackie and Pat my cross-eyed look. We started laughing like naughty children, which prompted a "shush" from Rebecca.

The third couple wasn't a couple at all, at least not in a romantic sense. They were a mother and son duo, and the son was Jonathan. "Beatrice Birnbaum," boomed the deep-voiced septuagenarian—a stunning, erect-postured, commanding woman who removed her sunglasses and squared her shoulders before she spoke, and gave off the sense that she was not to be crossed, despite having a big, wide smile plastered across her face. She had the shiniest silvery gray hair I'd ever seen, lacquered and expensively cut, with bangs across her forehead and layers framing her face. "My son Jonathan and I live in Palm Beach, but we come north in the summer to visit family and friends. Jonathan's an attorney who harbors ambitions of being a *chef*, of all things. I hope this week will disabuse him of that notion." She maintained the smile even as her tone suggested utter disdain for her son and his "notion."

We all glanced at Jonathan, who at forty-plus was old enough to make his own career decisions as well as stop traveling with his mother.

"Beatrice thinks I must be going through a mid-life crisis, and maybe I am, but there are worse things, right?" he said, with a jolly laugh that broke the tension and reinforced my interest in him as a potential romantic partner. I'd just have to wean him off his mommy. "The truth is, I'd really like to go to culinary school in my spare time and see what comes of it. Cooking farm-to-table food and feeding it to people seems like a creative and enjoyable pursuit."

"It is indeed," commented Rebecca. "A noble pursuit."

"I have a genuine appreciation for the work that's done here at Whitley," Beatrice allowed, still smiling incongruously. "And there's nothing I relish more than a meal prepared with the freshest ingredients and the utmost skill, but Jonathan's father, my dear Arthur, built that law firm. He'd turn over in his grave if he knew his only son was thinking of throwing it all away in order to make beet-and-goat-cheese salads."

As Jonathan winked at me as if to say, "Don't pay any attention to her," I decided to begin the weaning process immediately.

"I'm Elaine Zimmerman," I said. "I'm a senior account executive at Pearson & Strulley, the international PR firm, and I don't think I'm throwing it all away by taking a week off with my best friends, Beatrice." Her smile faded, and she glared at me. "I'm a complete klutz in the kitchen, and I couldn't tell you the difference between snap peas and snow peas, never mind whether that Belgian salad vegetable is pronounced en-dive or on-deev, but it'll be fun to watch good cooks like Jonathan work their magic."

"Thanks for the assist, Elaine," said Jonathan, giving me a grateful, knowing smile, as if we'd just gone through an ordeal together. "Something tells me you'll be out-cooking us all by the end of the week."

"I doubt that," I said, pleased that I had scored the compliment.

"Hi everyone," said Jackie. "I'm Jackie Gault and I run a nursery in Westchester County. I've logged lots of time in the garden, but farming is new to me. I'm really excited to cook what Whitley grows." She pumped her fist, just the way she did when her favorite baseball team won. She knew the names and stats of all the players, and could sit and stare at a game for hours. She deserved a boyfriend who would appreciate the jock in her. Isn't that what men wanted? A woman who shared their interests? I'd shared Simon's interests. We'd sent each other links to magazine pieces we liked and ran off to see buzz-worthy films as soon as they were released. We'd read the same books on our iPads and compared notes about them as soon as we were both done. A lot of good that did me.

"Hello, my name is Patricia Kovecky," said Pat, who rarely used her formal first name unless she was feeling insecure in front of a group. "My husband is Dr. William Kovecky." She lowered her eyes as she waited for the others to recognize that they were in the presence of Mrs. God of Gastroenterology. No one did. Again, I felt the need to jump in.

"Bill's a regular contributor on GMA," I said, jumping into publicist mode. "Brilliant gastroenterologist, which will come in handy if anyone eats dandelion greens and gets a bad case of the runs."

Jonathan laughed. He really was a likable person, the opposite of his mother, and I was glad he wasn't letting her spoil his trip. But Lake seized on my comment as if it were a major teachable moment.

"Dandelion greens are richer in beta carotene than carrots, and they provide valuable nutrients," she said with the zeal of an evangelical.

"We use the tender young greens in mesclun salads and smoothies," her life partner Gabriel added. "They should become part of your diet, Elaine."

My diet was none of their business. Evidently, they were going to be a chore.

Pat cleared her throat. "I have five teenaged children, and my youngest, Lucy, put on a few extra pounds in the past year. I didn't think too much of it until she came home from band practice one day—she plays the clarinet—and said two of the other girls called her fat. Well, you could have knocked me over with a fender when she told me that."

I was about to say, "It's *feather*, Pat," but kept my mouth shut for a change.

"So I'm interested in learning how to cook farm foods that will help Lucy lose weight the healthy way." She patted her tummy. "The same goes for her mother."

"I'm Alex Langer," said an attractive woman with flowing blonde locks, who was decked out in the style known as Boho chic. Her outfit involved an ivory top embroidered with butterflies and a matching bandana around her head, jeans with holes at the knees, gladiator sandals, and lots of interesting little chains and bracelets. The only deviation in her loose, laid-back look was the enormous rock on her left hand. I'm talking about a diamond that made my eyes bug out. She was about my age, I guessed, and showed the same signs of wear and tear, but she had two things I didn't: an engagement ring and a man who was ready to commit. "I live in the city and I'm here for two reasons," she continued. "I definitely want to improve my cooking skills. And I'm writing a screenplay about a chef, so this trip is research."

A screenplay? Was this a PR opportunity for Pearson & Strulley? Ever on the hunt for new clients, I asked, "Is it your first script, Alex, or have you written movies we've seen?" In other words, was there a studio that needed an Oscar campaign? I didn't work on those accounts personally, but we had an entire department that did.

"My first screenplay," she said proudly. "In my real life, I'm a dental hygienist."

Well, that part made sense. Her teeth were spectacularly white and straight. She probably got discounts on the braces and bleaching.

"My fiancé treated me to the week here," she explained. "He would have stayed after dropping me off, but he's got a business to run."

"He sounds like a catch," said Jackie with an envious laugh. "Does he have a brother?"

"He absolutely does," said Alex. "We'll talk." She had a warm and friendly air about her—something this group sorely needed.

"Well," said Rebecca, "I'm glad you all came to Whitley and hope the week delivers on your expectations, whatever they may be. We have lots to do today, so let's get moving. After I finish the guided tour of the farm, you're going to forage for wild edibles with Kevin, our gardener, and then spend the afternoon with Chef Hill, who'll teach you how to cook what you pulled out of the earth and much more."

"Jason Hill! Yay!" squealed Connie, who waved her arms in the air as if she were trying to beat back a colony of bats. "He challenged Michael Symon on *Iron Chef* a couple of years ago. He lost—the judges thought his rabbit risotto was too soupy—but I *love* him! The last time I saw him was when he came to Chicago, and he was the best!"

As Rebecca turned and began to lead us up a steep slope, toward a dense thicket of vegetation into which we would be foraging, Jackie grabbed me and said, "Is Connie a chef groupie or what?"

"She seems okay," I said, "one of those comfortable-in-her-own-skin people who follows her bliss, to pile on the clichés. Same with Alex."

"Jonathan is such a gentleman," said Pat, "and a very devoted son."

"He's probably loaded," said Jackie. "I didn't hear anything about a wife, by the way."

"I bet he had one, but Mommy Dearest bumped her off so she could have him all to herself," I said.

"*Elaine.*" Jackie groaned. "No murderers on this trip, remember?"

4

"What you'll be seeing are the kinds of plants you'll find around farms, around manure piles, around compost piles—agricultural settings where there's disturbed soil," said Kevin Koontz, Whitley's forager-in-chief, a thin, serious man who wore a denim shirt, jeans, a wide-brimmed straw hat, and a handkerchief. If he'd been chewing on a blade of grass, I would have cast him in a dinner theater production of *Oklahoma*. "You might also find them among the weeds in your own garden or your neighbor's. Here's an example."

As he yanked one of the weeds out of the ground, I wiped a gallon of sweat off my face. After what had felt like an endless hike, we'd stopped under a shady grove—a respite.

"It's amaranth," he said, passing around sprigs of a green-leafed plant I couldn't tell from basil or a thousand others. "The leaves are incredibly nutritious, packed with vitamins and protein. That being said, it absorbs nitrogen, robbing oxygen from your body, so you can experience some toxicity if you consume too much of it."

I raised my hand. "Toxicity?" Why were we paying so much money to forage for supposedly edible foods that could poison us?

"You don't gorge on it," said Lake. "You just use it in cooking the way you'd use other greens. Like sorrel."

Sorrel schmorrel. I had a terrible urge to punch Lake Vanderkloot-Arnold in the face, but she was so emaciated I could probably just breathe on her and she'd fall over.

"I'm not trying to scare anybody," said Kevin. "I just want you all to be aware that it's not healthy to eat pounds and pounds of amaranth. If you watch sheep graze, you see that they're foraging, eating a little bit of this and a little bit of that. We should follow their example."

"That's what my cardiologist tells me," Ronnie said, followed by a loud belch, one of those burps that start out as a hiccup. "Eat a little bit of this and a little bit of that, have smaller portions and skip the visits to Olive Garden for their all-you-can-eat pasta."

"You seriously *go* to that place?" Gabriel said, his expression registering pure revulsion. "Their food is antithetical to everything about farm-to-table."

Ronnie shrugged. "It comes from a farm somewhere. And it sure tastes good for the price. I have a nice little nest egg, but that doesn't mean I can't try to save a buck when I'm hungry."

"Lake mentioned sorrel, and we just happen to have some," Kevin went on, bending down to pull more weeds out of the ground and pass them around. I noticed that Jackie was trailing right behind him, no doubt interested in him as a sexual partner.

"Sorrel's a really good diuretic," said Gabriel, who

between the diuretics and the inevitable juices probably peed every six seconds. "Everyone should add it to their diet."

"And here are highbush blueberries," said Kevin, pointing to a tangle of plants I actually recognized. "Feel free to enjoy some while we talk."

Everyone reached for the little purple berries and popped them into their mouths except me. Weren't we supposed to wash fruit thoroughly before eating it?

Kevin led us deeper into the heart of darkness where he picked, discussed, and passed around samples of lamb's-quarter, chocolate mint, purslane, and many other varieties of plants that we were to add to our culinary repertoires. I have to admit that I did find the foraging expedition educational in the same way that any sort of travel is broadening, and I was open to eating weeds if they were really so healthy, but I didn't have a farm in my apartment, you know? I didn't have a backyard either, or even those tiny containers of herbs that people put on their windowsill. I didn't have plants, period, because they always withered and died from too much water or not enough, and I'd feel like a failure every time I carted a dead philodendron to the trash.

"Elaine, want to sample this one?" Jonathan asked, sidling up next to me and offering me one of the weeds.

"Sure, thanks," I said. It tasted like the sort of bitter, too-tough-to-chew garnishes I always left on the side of the plate, but what I did enjoy was the way the tips of Jonathan's fingers gracefully brushed my lips as he fed me. It was a very intimate gesture, and I would have blushed if I'd been the type.

"Did you sleep well last night?" he asked, his brown eyes boring into me with laser focus. I always heard that there were men who could make you feel as if you were the only one in the room (or in the woods, in this case), and Jonathan Birnbaum had that gift.

"Yes, I conked right out," I said. "You?"

"I had a dream about you," he said. "We were in Palm Beach swimming in my pool. You were doing the breast stroke, as I remember."

"Sadly, the dog paddle is the only stroke I know." So he was imagining me in a bikini or perhaps as a skinny-dipper—doing the *breast*stroke.

"At the risk of repeating myself, I'm really glad you're here, Elaine," he said. "Something tells me you're going to make this trip a memorable week for me."

"Oh, come on. You probably say that to all the women who come to cultivate their bounties."

He laughed. "Only the ones whose bounties are worth cultivating."

"Help! Help!" came a shout from behind us. "I fell!"

We turned to find the shout, and it belonged to Beatrice. She was lying flat on her back in the bushes, moaning. She must have slipped on a rock or a branch.

Jonathan hurried to her side with me in tow. Amazingly, every strand of her shiny silvery gray hair was still in place, even her bangs, and there was no evidence of blood or torn clothing. Still, she was in her seventies, and bones were brittle at that age. My mother had her original hips, knees, and teeth—her marbles too—but it was a crapshoot.

"Can you tell me where it hurts, Mother?" Jonathan asked. He lowered himself to the ground and sat next to her.

"Try not to move, Beatrice," said Kevin, our forager. "Let's be sure you're not injured."

As everyone gathered around and murmured their concern for a member of our newly formed group, Jackie whispered, "I love the way Kevin's taking charge. He has a cute ass, too."

"*Ow*," Beatrice wailed, ignoring Kevin's warning and grabbing and clinging to her son's hand and twisting her body in his direction, nearly dragging him down with her. "I think it's my back."

"So you didn't break a hip or anything?" said Jonathan.

"I don't think so," she said, grimacing and wincing and making every pained face I'd ever seen, creating quite the theatrical experience. "My back is sore."

"It's always sore," he said gently. "You have arthritis, Mother."

Pat whispered, "Do you think she's faking? Lucy fakes stomachaches when she doesn't want to go to gym class."

"Anything's possible," I said.

"More than possible," said Jackie. "She probably saw her son coming on to you, Elaine, and got jealous."

Kevin told Beatrice to lie back down and then asked her to rate her pain level on a scale from one to ten.

"My back's a ten," she said between moans.

"I'll call for the EMTs," he said. "Once they get you to the hospital, the doctors will be able to diagnose—"

"I am not going to any hospitals!" Imperious Beatrice had quickly replaced Vulnerable Beatrice.

"It's just a precaution," said Kevin. "If everything checks out, they'll let you come right back here."

"Nonsense," she said. "My son will make sure I'm all right. Help me up, Jonathan, would you, dear?"

He didn't contradict her, as if he'd been through this

routine before and knew it would be a waste of time. Instead, he held her hand and carefully pulled her to her feet, while we all stood there watching, a rapt audience.

Beatrice gave us a triumphant wave, like a soldier limping off the battlefield after having been wounded in combat. She arched an eyebrow when she lit on me and said, "My son will take good care of me now."

Before Jonathan began their walk back to solid ground, he leaned toward me and said, "Welcome to my world. Please don't let it scare you off."

"I don't scare easily," I said. I was lying, of course. I scared easily and often, but there was something about the way Jonathan had handled his mother that impressed me. He was sweet and kind and did what she'd asked, but without seeming reduced or resentful.

"I'm counting on it," he said with a wink.

"Wow, he likes you." Jackie nudged me after they were gone.

"He does," Pat agreed. "Now aren't you glad you came this week?"

"We'll see," I said. "I only just met him, let's not forget. But no matter what happens between us, it's good to be in the country, ninety miles away from you know who."

My friends didn't answer, I assumed, because deep down they were still rooting for Team Simon—a fruitless enterprise.

5

Rebecca handed each of us a Whitley chef's apron and instructed us to sit in the folding chairs arranged in two rows of five, facing the center countertop that functioned as a stage. I took a seat in the front row; Pat and Jackie sat on either side of me.

"This demo kitchen's a lot nicer than mine," said Jackie, who was renting the guesthouse on the estate of one of her longtime landscaping customers. She lived rent free in exchange for tending to the customer's gardens, and the only downside was a kitchen the size of a closet.

"It's nicer than most people's," I agreed.

One of Whitley's red barns had been converted into a state-of-the-art facility with high-end appliances, lots of countertop workspaces, and a separate alcove for a long oak dining table with chairs on either side. The table had been set for eleven, so I assumed we'd be sitting down to eat whatever it was we were about to cook. I would have known exactly what the menu was if I'd bothered to sort through the Whitley tote bag I'd picked up at the Welcome Happy Hour, but I'd dumped it somewhere in the cottage and forgotten about it.

"Chef Hill, our artisan in residence, will arrive any minute," Rebecca said. "He's a busy man, and we're lucky to have him whenever he gets here."

"He's so worth waiting for!" Connie said, flapping her arms again from the end of our row.

"I hope she doesn't jump up and start screaming when he gets here," Jackie muttered. "She's like a teenybopper at a Justin Bieber concert."

Jonathan, who was sitting directly behind us, leaned forward and whispered, nodding at Connie, "She's very enthusiastic, isn't she?"

I turned around and smiled at him. He smiled back. It was fun flirting with a hot guy in a cooking class, especially because I was newly on the market and hadn't flirted in a while. Men you hardly know are exciting in that there's no stored data of the same inane arguments, no baggage to contend with. Well, okay, Jonathan had Beatrice, who was probably heavier baggage than a Louis Vuitton trunk.

"For those who haven't had a chance to read his bio," Rebecca stood next to the counter, tapping her fingers on it, unable to contain her excitement, "Jason Hill became a leader in the creative, clean-food, farm-to-table movement with the launch of The Grow, his flagship restaurant in Manhattan's Hell's Kitchen. You each got a complimentary copy of his most recent cookbook, *The Grow Eats*, in your tote bag last night. His other two cookbooks are available for purchase in our gift shop. A devoted husband and father of two, Chef Hill is a frequent competitor and judge on television cooking shows and appears at food and wine events around the world. He's the owner-chef of six outposts of The Grow, the cornerstone of his Planetary Empire Corporation whose mission is to cook and serve food that's grown responsibly and sustainably, to support farm workers' rights, and to make ingredient choices based on the environment as well as flavor. Currently, he's scouting locations for his next eatery."

"He needs to put it in Wisconsin!" Connie shouted. "Wouldn't that be the best, Ronnie?"

He patted her considerable thigh. "Maybe we'd get a discount since you've been to so many of his talks."

"I've never heard of him," Pat whispered with an apologetic shrug. "The only TV chef I know is Julia Child."

"Unfortunately, she won't be coming this week," I said.

"I'm thinking of basing my main character on Jason Hill," said Alex, who was seated next to Jackie. "My script is about a chef who loses his restaurant to his young, ambitious sous-chef—only to find that the sous-chef is also angling to steal his wife. It's *All About Eve* with a foodie twist."

"Don't give up your day job," I wanted to say but didn't, because Alex seemed like a decent person. "Sounds fascinating," I said instead. "Have you always wanted to be a screenwriter?"

"Any kind of writer," she said. "You should see all the novels and short stories I've started and never finished."

"Maybe this script is the one," I said. "If it sells, you can turn it into a novel."

"I wish." She smiled hopefully. "Then I can give up dentistry and write full-time. Removing tartar from people's teeth gets old after a while."

I was about to share my own trials with crowns and root canals and receding gums, but I noticed that Rebecca was hurrying into the hall outside the kitchen. I assumed she was retrieving Chef Hill so she could usher him in with great fanfare. I turned away to resume my conversation with Alex when I heard an oddly familiar voice coming from the hall, a male voice, a voice that was apologizing to Rebecca for being late.

"I meant to get here earlier, but hey, circumstances beyond my control and all that," the male voice went on, becoming more identifiable—too identifiable—with every syllable.

It can't be, I thought. It really couldn't be, even though Simon often used the fallback line, "Hey, circumstances beyond my control and all that," when he was late. No. It was impossible, unthinkable, unconscionable that he would suddenly appear at Whitley Farm—as a Cultivate Our Bounty agritourist, no less. No. Just no. I must have been overthinking it.

"Not a problem," Rebecca said.

"No, really," said the voice. "One of these days I'll show up on time. Being late is a weakness of mine, a character flaw."

This can't be happening, I thought. Yes, Simon was always late for things, but so were plenty of other people. On the other hand, he was probably the record-holder for being late, and I had the emotional scars to prove it. Take my birthday, for instance, which turned out to be the last straw for our relationship. He'd made a reservation at my favorite restaurant. He'd said we'd have a romantic evening, just the two of us, and that he'd bought a special present for me—a present that he'd wait to give me after we got home from dinner, a present that would have significance for us as a couple. I thought that he didn't want to make a big show of proposing at the restaurant because it was such a cliché the way men slipped rings in champagne glasses and hid them in bread baskets and arranged for pastry chefs to embed them in the center of chocolate molten lava cakes. I really thought he meant business.

Our reservation for dinner on that fateful night was for seven thirty. I didn't panic when he didn't show up at my apartment at six thirty. I didn't panic when he didn't show up at seven, either. I didn't even panic when he didn't show at seven fifteen, although the restaurant was on the West Side and I lived on the East Side. And it was pouring so hard we'd never in a million years be able to get a cab. Oh, and the restaurant was one of those self-important places that charged your credit card if you bailed at the last minute. I reminded myself that Simon was habitually late and had been since I'd met him on the ship when he used to arrive at dinner every night at least ten minutes after the rest of us were seated. He was forever losing track of time, and I'd learned over the course of our many months together that his intractable tardiness was simply a personality quirk. I loved him in spite of his lateness is what I'm saying.

But when he walked into my apartment at 8:34, toting a heavily soaked, gift-wrapped package as big as a microwave, I was beyond livid. I was livid that he was late on a night that was supposed to be one of the happiest nights of my life. I was livid that our reservation was canceled and I wouldn't be swooning over the restaurant's pan roasted loup de mer with the crispy skin, the potato puree, or the lemon artichoke sauce. I was livid—and this was the most egregious item on the already egregious list—that the heavily soaked, gift-wrapped package as big as a microwave turned out to be a microwave. I mean, you can't put a microwave on the ring finger of your left hand and go around modeling it for everybody now can you?

"I'm sorry you missed our welcome party last night and our foraging expedition this morning," said Rebecca. "Come and join the others while we wait for Chef Hill to get here."

I started sweating like some crazed menopausal woman off her HRT, and if volcanic lava could explode out of one's nose and ears, it would have exploded out of mine.

"Really looking forward to these cooking classes," said the voice.

"You'll have a great time," said Rebecca. "Follow me."

He doesn't have the balls, I thought as I heard the footsteps approaching. *He has no right to crash my week with my friends. I've already begun to entertain the possibility of a relationship with Jonathan Birnbaum. I've moved on!*

I ducked as they entered the kitchen. My right eyelid began to twitch too, one of those nerve things where you lose control of your body and can't do a thing about it. I finally glanced up, only because I couldn't spend the whole class with my chin tucked inside my rib cage, and confirmed that our latecomer for the week, the entire fucking week, was my former boyfriend.

Naturally, he looked stupidly handsome in his jeans and Ralph Lauren Polo shirt, the mesh slim-fit one with the breathable cotton, the one in that liquid-blue shade that accentuated his liquid-blue eyes. The one he'd worn on the ship last year when he'd made me fall in love with him. He had the nerve to wear that shirt of all shirts. But he could have worn one of Whitley's tote bags and still looked movie-star handsome—George Clooney, Cary Grant handsome, only extremely tall, around six five, which made us the perfect couple, height-wise. He had dark, wavy hair with touches of gray at his temples, sky-blue eyes behind his tortoiseshell glasses, a straight nose, a square jaw, juicy lips, a lean, yet broad-shouldered body, the complete visual package.

He waved at me with a grin that should have been sheepish but was instead full of self-confidence and good cheer, and took a seat in the row behind me, next to Beatrice, who seemed to have recovered just fine from her "fall." I heard him introduce himself to her and everybody else. He told them his grandparents used to have a farm up in Duchess County and as a boy he'd enjoyed spending weekends there. He regaled them with tales of collecting eggs from the chickens and feeding the baby goats with a bottle and watching Rudy, the rooster, wander into the driveway and nearly get run over by his grandpa Charlie's tractor. So what if he'd told me the same stories and they were true? He had walked right into my vacation, my cooking class, my space, and charmed the crap out of these people; it was a total breach of breakup etiquette.

Keeping my gaze straight ahead, I reached for Jackie's hand with my right, Pat's hand with my left, and hissed, "Do you believe this?" When all they did was giggle, I realized I'd been set up. "You knew?" I hissed some more, searching their faces now. "You *knew*?"

Jackie leaned in and whispered, "He wants to show you he's sorry. He asked us if it was okay to come and we said yes."

I felt a hand on my shoulder. I didn't turn around.

"Hey, Slim," said Simon.

"You think this is funny," I said still looking straight ahead.

"A little," he agreed. "I can't wait to see you cooking. It'll be epic."

Ha ha ha. I'd give him epic. An epic week of the cold shoulder.

I was relieved when Chef Jason Hill materialized in his chef whites with his entourage of four, each of whom was a young male schlepping a heavy, clanging bag of kitchen tools. He waved halfheartedly at us with the pained expression of a very famous person who resented having to perform in front of such a small audience.

Connie bolted up, threw her arms in the air and said, "He's heeeere!" and Chef Hill didn't so much as make eye contact with her. A compact man in his mid thirties, with tattoos that ran up his neck and down the exposed parts of his arms, he had a crooked, tough-guy nose, acne-scarred skin, a shaved head, and a goatee—not a heartthrob in the conventional sense but the sort of anti-hero that culinary stars were made of these days. He reeked of pomposity as he issued commands to the members of his staff, who proceeded to prep all sorts of food with lightning speed, as if their boss had a plane to catch.

While we students continued to sit in our seats, and Rebecca wished us an enjoyable class before fleeing, he barked more orders at the underlings and then looked up at us and said, "Hold tight, gang. Be right back," after which he disappeared in the direction of the restroom. When he returned a few minutes later, his mood seemed to have lightened. Even from my seat I could guess why: His nostrils were dusted with the tiniest traces of a powder that wasn't confectioner's sugar, and he was sniffling.

"I think Chef Hill's a cokehead," I whispered to Pat and Jackie. "It would give new meaning to farm-to-table, as in a farm in Colombia."

"But sodas are bad for you," said Pat. "Even I know that."

"She means cocaine, Pat," said Jackie. "It's just Elaine being Elaine."

"It could be true," I said. "The guy promotes clean food, but if he's polluting his own body then he's a phony." I was about to defend my theory, but Chef Hill began our class by stepping out from behind the counter and walking quickly toward us.

"I'll tell you one thing," said Jackie. "He's not nearly as hot in person. I'm much more into Kevin, our forager. Now there's a guy I'd like to—"

"I'm Jason Hill," he said with a rapid-fire delivery, as if the coke had somehow sped up his vocal chords along with his brain. "Hope all you people are ready to cook from the land today. Do you know how to get the best flavor out of food? I'll tell you how: Get it from farmers who are local. That's right. Get it from someone in the neighborhood, someone whose growing practices you respect. As a cook, you'll be the curators of what tastes good, of what's delicious, and the way to get 'delicious' is to get it fresh. Look, I'll be honest. My family is the world to me. They keep me grounded. They're my emotional and spiritual center. Feeding them clean, farm-to-table, dock-to-dish meals is the same as telling them I love them. So here's the deal. I can show you people every recipe and technique ever created, but it all starts with freshness, with purity, with saving our planet by not dumping chemicals on what we put in our mouths."

Chef Hill nodded at us to indicate his little speech was over, and Lake and Gabriel, clearly his acolytes, leapt to their feet and clapped vigorously, which made everybody else feel obligated to leap to their feet and clap vigorously.

"Thanks, thanks," said Chef Hill, gesturing for us to sit back down. "Now, just so I have an idea what I'm dealing with this week, how many of you think you know your way around the kitchen, knife skills and all?"

Lake and Gabriel raised their hands and announced that they had their own set of knives at home with their initials on them. Jonathan raised his hand and said he found cooking to be a very satisfying experience. Alex raised her hand and said she enjoyed cooking but was intimidated by recipes with more than six ingredients. Pat lifted her hand and said she cooked for her children but that she often fell back on mac and cheese, sloppy joes, and Mrs. Paul's frozen fish sticks. And Connie raised her hand and said she'd met Chef Hill before—several times, in fact—and bought all his cookbooks in both print and e-book editions, which didn't qualify as knowing how to cook but got him to glance in her direction. Simon didn't raise his hand but took the opportunity to lean over and say to me, "You should have told him about the turkey you roasted at Thanksgiving, Slim. Remember how you left the plastic bag of giblets in there and the plastic melted?"

Yes, hilarious. Good one, Simon. I'd like to roast your bag of giblets.

"I'm splitting you into groups by mixing up the know-hows and the wannabes," he said. "Then I'll assign everybody tasks—bang bang."

"Bang bang," I would come to learn, was Chef Hill's catchphrase, the way Emeril became synonymous with "Bam," and he used it as liberally as he used salt. He sent me, Jonathan, Ronnie, and Gabriel over to a table on which rested two long slabs of meat. They were pork tenderloins that looked like a couple of extremely large penises, pink and glistening under the recessed lighting.

I waved across the room to Jackie, who had gathered with Connie and Alex over what looked like salad and vegetable fixings, and at Pat, poor thing, who'd been exiled to the dessert station with Lake, Beatrice, and Simon, who thought I was waving to him even though I was doing anything but.

"Oh, boy, do I love this animal," said Ronnie, salivating over the raw meat, which was probably rife with trichinosis.

"According to the background material we got for each recipe, these tenderloins come directly from Whitley's pasture," said Gabriel. "They're grass-fed and low in fat."

"I haven't looked in my tote bag," I confessed. "I don't even remember where I put it. Is the recipe very difficult?"

"Not if you follow the directions," he said. "Cooking is like working out at the gym: discipline, discipline, discipline."

"You'll be fine, Elaine," said Jonathan with a reassuring smile. "If you have a question, just ask me."

"Here I am," said Chef Hill as he scuttled over to us, his shortness keeping him low to the ground like a crawling insect. "You guys are making the main course, which is pork tenderloin stuffed with prosciutto, pesto, and arugula. Now let's get at this—bang bang." He snapped his fingers and the members of his entourage rushed over with bowls of ingredients. "You first." He nodded at me. "What's your name, hon?"

Hon. Did this man not have as much respect for workplace protocol as he did for responsibly fertilized soil? "My name is Elaine," I said, trying to keep the edge out of my voice. "I'm inexperienced in the kitchen, just so you know."

"We'll have you cooking like a pro, hon." He motioned me closer to the cutting board. "You're going to butterfly these babies after you cut off the silver skin—bang bang."

I assumed he would demonstrate what the hell he was talking about, but he stood there waiting for me to do what I was told. When neither of us moved for several awkward seconds, Jonathan jumped in and took over, rescuing me just like I'd rescued him earlier. He picked up one of the six knives on the table and began peeling back the layer of fat on the two tenderloins.

"Yeah, that's how it's done," said Chef Hill. "Perfect execution. Can you butterfly these too, guy?"

"Sure."

Clearly, Jonathan was a ringer. With care and skill, he reached for another knife and, holding the blade flat so it was parallel to the meat, he cut across the pork nearly to the opposite end, and then opened the flaps as you would a book. Covering the tenderloins with plastic wrap, he pounded them with a mallet to make them thinner, and looked up at our chef. "Next step?"

"Next step is you get your own restaurant, guy," he said, slapping Jonathan on the back. "You've got talent. Well done." He pointed at Gabriel. "You're up."

Gabriel's job was to spread a piece of prosciutto on

top of each butterflied and flattened tenderloin, then make the pesto.

"No biggie, right, guy?" said Chef Hill, thumping Gabriel on the back. "All you do is throw everything into the processor and pulse."

Into the food processor went shelled pistachios, figs, chopped garlic, basil, freshly grated Parmesan cheese, and olive oil. Gabriel mixed it all up, then stood back from the machine admiring his work.

"Now you again, hon," Chef Hill said to me. He didn't slap me on the back, but he did give me a little shove I didn't appreciate. "Spread the pesto on top of the pork, then mound it with the arugula."

Okay, Elaine. This isn't brain surgery, I told myself. This is cooking, which is what people all across the world do in rooms called kitchens. I thought of my mother, who cooked but inattentively. I remembered when I was kid, and she was making me macaroni and cheese for dinner. She was stirring it on the stove when the phone rang. It was her older sister, my Aunt Rhoda. Theirs was a fraught sibling relationship, involving long periods in which they refused to speak to each other for reasons no one understood. My mother was so undone by the call that she forgot about the macaroni and cheese and pretty much incinerated it. Is it any wonder I never learned how to cook?

"Come on, hon!" Chef Hill snapped, checking his watch. "You're holding up the works."

"Sorry." I made a mental note to go on Yelp, Urbanspoon, and TripAdvisor and trash Chef Hill for being a rotten cooking instructor.

I picked up a spatula and poured the pesto on top of

the prosciutto laid out over the butterflied schlongs, and spread it around. Then I reached for the arugula leaves and deposited them onto the meat.

"See? That wasn't anything to get all wigged out about," said the cokehead.

"No, it really wasn't." I smiled, thinking of all the nasty things I would write about him online.

"You're up, guy," he said, motioning Jonathan toward the meat. "Since you're the star in this group, how about you fold these babies up, tie them with the string, sear them nice and brown on all sides in the skillet, and finish them off in the oven while I go help the others." And off he went in Jackie's direction.

"I guess we're free to eat the leftovers," said Ronnie, who emitted one of his hiccup-belches, then reached into the bowl of pistachios and crammed handfuls of them into his mouth. When he'd emptied the bowl of nuts, he grazed on the arugula, getting most of it stuck between his teeth. "I think I'll go see how Cupcake is doing."

After Ronnie had waddled over to his wife's station, Jonathan said, "Cupcake is probably thrilled that she's breathing Chef Hill's air." We shared a laugh. "Not very warm and fuzzy, our chef."

"No, but hey, you're good with food, Jonathan," I said. "You have a natural feel for it, and maybe you really should pursue it as a career. It's never too late for reinvention." Like I knew about reinvention. I wore the same pale pink nail polish color year after year. Never changed it, not even when women started painting their nails in blood reds and teal blues and pewter grays. I resisted change the way cats resist baths.

"You're a very supportive person, Elaine," said Jonathan. "I don't get much of that from my mother."

"What about the rest of your family?" I asked, instead of coming right out and grilling him about his marital status and/or sexual orientation.

"I'm an only child, and my mother's dependence on me got worse after my father died. I'm all she has, and since my latest divorce—there have been two—she's afraid I'll leave Palm Beach and run off to some foodie mecca in Brooklyn."

"Everybody says Queens is the new Brooklyn. Maybe you should go there and bring her with you."

"God no." He laughed. "I take yearly trips with her. I spend Sunday afternoons with her. I handle her financial affairs and put in appearances at her charity functions, but that's my limit. I lead my own life." He sounded relieved to get all that off his chest. "Tell me about you? Married? Significant other? Still on the market? None of the above?"

A loaded question, given the circumstances. "I was divorced—once—from a businessman named Eric Zucker. He runs a chain of funeral homes in the Tri-State area. Right after we were married, he started sleeping with Lola, the employee who applies industrial strength makeup to the embalmed corpses. According to my therapist, I had essentially married my father, who was always shtupping redheads behind my mother's back. When I was twelve, he found one who—quote unquote—'really rang his chimes.' He abandoned us for her and never looked back."

"Must have been tough to deal with on both counts," said Jonathan. "If it's any consolation, I've got my own war stories. We'll have a drink and see whose are worse. What about now?"

"For the drink?" We were in the middle of a cooking class.

"No, what about now in terms of any significant other? Is there a boyfriend?"

"Oh, that," I said as if Simon were no big deal and not watching us from a few yards away. "I'm newly single after ending a relationship."

"Good," he said. "So there's a window of opportunity."

"For what?" I said, fishing. I found Jonathan more than a little appealing, and there was no harm in getting to know him better.

"For seeing how this goes," he said, pointing to himself and then to me. "It's not everyday that I meet a woman willing to stand up to the formidable Beatrice Birnbaum. My ex-wives either cowered in her presence or avoided her altogether."

"Hey, I'm a pushy New Yorker," I said. "We mug the muggers."

He laughed again. "I was born in the city, but I've lived in Florida since I was ten, the year my father decided he hated winter. I miss it up here. I'd move back in a minute. Maybe we'll fall in love and you'll beg me to move back."

"Tell me the truth: Do you say things like that to every woman you meet on vacation?"

"No, but I like pretending I do. It's all part of my smooth-and-sophisticated act. Is it working?"

"It might be." It was fun trading rom-com retorts instead of stuffing pork tenderloins. "Would you really move back to New York though? What about your—"

I couldn't finish the sentence because a very loud "Goddammit!" bellowed from across the room.

"What now?" said Jonathan. We looked in the direction

of the commotion to find that Chef Hill was grabbing his finger and hopping around as if he'd been set on fire. "At least it's not my mother this time."

It turned out that Jackie, Alex, and Connie had been assigned both the amaranth soup and the bulgur-wheat-and-wild-blueberry salad, and that somewhere along the way there had been an incident.

"Missed it," Jackie said with a helpless shrug, when I was breathless to know what had happened.

"I did too," said Alex. "I was folding the blueberries into the bulgur, and Jackie was making the vinaigrette. She was asking about my fiancé's brother, and I was telling her he might be ready to date again after a bad breakup."

"I didn't do it on purpose, Chef Hill!" Connie was protesting, her pudgy cheeks scarlet, arms flailing. "I swear I didn't!" She seemed on the verge of a psychotic break.

"Damn right she didn't," Ronnie said in defense of his wife.

"Well, I sure as shit didn't do it to myself," said the chef, who yelled for an underling to help. Blood was gushing from the forefinger on his right hand despite his having wrapped it in a kitchen towel. "She could have hacked me to death."

I'm sorry to report that my first thought was not for the chef's health and wellbeing. It was for my own. I vowed not to let a single molecule of the soup cross my lips, not when there was a possibility that his bodily fluid had contaminated it, and not unless someone made a fresh batch after the cutting board had been scrupulously scrubbed.

"I was just trying to do my best!" Connie cried. "I wanted to please you."

"You said you had knife skills, for Christ's sake," Chef

Hill muttered, while a young man with a ponytail and black stainless steel studs in his earlobes wrapped a bandage around his boss's injured finger. "I was demonstrating how to chop the amaranth because you didn't have a clue and neither did the other ladies. But did they crowd me at the cutting board? No. Did they get in my space? No. Did they grab a serrated bread knife and start chopping amaranth where my finger was? No. I mean who *does* that?"

"Listen, buddy, she didn't mean to hurt you," said Ronnie, puffing out his chest with indignation. "She has all your cookbooks. She wouldn't hurt anybody."

"She's just a little…eager," Jonathan chimed in, proving once again that he was chivalrous. "Why don't I start from scratch on the amaranth soup, since I've read the recipe for it?"

"Fine," said Chef Hill. "I owe you, guy." He slapped Jonathan on the back with his uninjured hand.

"You're good to go," the medic underling told his boss. "Looks like a superficial wound, no stitches necessary."

"Just keep that one away from me," Chef Hill said, nodding at Connie.

"It was an accident!" she said emphatically, her tone angrier now, less pleading. "It's not like I tried to kill you!"

6

"I can't believe we made all this." Pat dove into the strawberry crumble a la mode that she, Lake, Beatrice, and Simon had concocted, including the ice cream that had come straight from Whitley's prized, grass-fed, hormone-free milking cows. Pat hadn't been able to operate the ice cream machine, and her first crack at it had yielded a substance with the consistency of cement, but Lake, who owned her own machine along with her immersion blender, her milk frother, and her molecular gastronomy set, took over and turned out a restaurant-quality product. I should add that the ice cream flavor wasn't chocolate or vanilla or anything as uninspired as that. No, it was hay. That's right. They made hay ice cream. Chef Hill delivered a big speech about the earthiness and grassiness of hay's aroma and flavor profile and the sustainability of incorporating it into the foods we'd be cooking during the week. If you asked me, it didn't smell earthy or grassy; it smelled like cannabis. As for Simon's contribution to the dessert, I really couldn't say. I ignored him. He tried to sit next to me at the long table where we were all partaking in the fruits of our labor, but I beckoned Jonathan over and he pulled out the empty chair next to me instead. Simon was stuck at the end, sandwiched between Ronnie and Connie.

"Alex and I did a pretty decent job with the bulgur salad," said Jackie, high-fiving her new friend.

"Yes, but I think we should all drink a toast to Jonathan," I said, both because I meant it and because I intended to make an ostentatious point of showing Simon I wasn't the least bit impressed that he'd dropped everything at the magazine so he could come to Connecticut and torture me. "To Jonathan." I raised my glass of Whitney's chardonnay. I'd been sipping it because it was all we were served, but I hated chardonnay. It was like licking the bark of an oak tree.

"To Jonathan," Jackie replied, not waiting for the rest of my toast before taking a healthy swallow of her wine. She was on her third glass and had asked one of Rebecca's assistants to bring us another bottle. I'm not saying she couldn't hold her liquor—she'd always been more of a drinker than I was—but she never used to drink so much so fast. Whenever I suggested she might want to slow down, she either teased me for being a worrier or told me to go fuck myself.

"Jonathan not only carried the heavy load on the pork tenderloin," I continued, my glass still in the air, "but the amaranth soup I was dreading was really tasty. He could be a professional chef, no question."

Beatrice's wingspan smile curled into a tight circle. "Please don't encourage him, dear. It's splendid that he has a hobby, but he's an attorney."

Jonathan laughed her off and hoisted his wineglass. "Thank you, Elaine. I appreciate the plug. When I'm running that kitchen in Queens that we talked about, I'll hire you to do my PR."

"Deal," I said and glanced at Simon, who had the nerve to mouth the words "I love you."

"I'd just like to express my gratitude to the land," said Lake, who spoke with her head down and her palms pressed together as if saying grace at a church breakfast. "We cultivated our bounty here today and it was a beautiful process, thanks to the guidance of our brilliant chef."

"Some chef," growled the normally good-natured Ronnie. "Jason Hill was not a nice person, the way he treated my cupcake."

Connie beamed. She'd bounced back from her ordeal by the end of the meal, she and Ronnie having gone back for several helpings of everything. "He'd better not mess with my hubby again," she said. "Ronnie's a teddy bear if he likes you, but he's a grizzly if he doesn't."

"I hope he really, really, really likes me then," said Pat, who was an even cheaper drunk than I was. One look at alcohol and she got a contact high, and from the flush on her face it was clear she'd had more than a look.

After the meal, Jackie and Alex were saying they wanted to adjourn to Whitley's bar for a nightcap. Pat was saying she wanted to go back to her cottage for a good night's sleep. Jonathan and I were saying we wanted to step outside and walk off all that food, and Simon took my elbow, apologized to Jonathan for interrupting our conversation, and said, "We need to talk."

"No," I said, wresting my arm from his grasp. "We really don't."

"Come on, Slim," he said as I turned back to Jonathan. "Give me twenty minutes. Your cottage or mine?"

"Not interested," I said. "Enjoy the rest of your evening."

"Do you two know each other?" asked Jonathan when it was clear Simon wasn't moving away. "From before, I mean."

"We do," I said with a casual, no-big-deal toss of the head. "I met Simon on last year's trip with Jackie and Pat. We were on a Caribbean cruise, and he was covering it for *Away from It All*, the travel magazine. Now it turns out that he's here covering agritourism vacations. Coincidence, right?"

"Maybe I'll put you both in my article," said Simon in an effort to play along, before taking my elbow again and spinning me around to face him. "Twenty minutes. That's all I ask."

"Five," I said.

"Fifteen," he said.

"Ten," I said.

"Ten it is," he said, and began to hustle me out of the kitchen.

"See you bright and early tomorrow," I called out to a mystified Jonathan. "Sleep well!"

7

We didn't go inside either of our cottages because I thought better of it. Trying to have a serious discussion when there was a big, poufy bed around would have invited temptation. So we spent his allotted ten minutes on the quaint front porch of my cottage sitting stiffly in the two Adirondack chairs. Whitley had thoughtfully outfitted the chairs with little rectangular lumbar support pillows. And yes, there was also a hammock on the porch, but it would have invited the same temptation as the bed, albeit with more swinging action.

"Nothing like country air, huh?" said Simon after a deep inhale. "Makes you think about moving out of the city, buying a house, and settling down."

"Not me," I said, smacking a mosquito that had landed on my neck. "Makes me think about catching the West Nile Virus." If that was his idea of a marriage proposal, he could shove it.

"I think Chef Hill is a cokehead, by the way," he said.

"Did you notice how he kept ducking out of the kitchen and coming back with more *energy*?"

"Yes, I did notice. Is that what you dragged me back here to talk about?"

"Look, Slim. I know you're still mad about your birthday dinner and I get it," he said. "Did I ever tell you I was a late baby? My mother had to carry me in her womb for almost nine-and-a-half months, and even then I took twenty hours to greet the world. I was born with the late gene, I guess. I should go to the Mayo Clinic. They must have developed a vaccine for chronically late people by now, right?"

I stared at him in the soft, dimming light of the setting sun. He was so handsome and so clueless. "This is all one big joke to you."

He shook his head, feigning remorse. "I shouldn't have said that about the Mayo Clinic. It's the Cleveland Clinic that probably has the vaccine."

I grabbed the lumbar support pillow from behind my back and threw it at his head. I missed, naturally, and it landed in a thicket of hydrangeas.

"I'm not in the mood for jokes or games or whatever it is you need to do to protect yourself from genuine feelings, Simon," I said. "I'm done with that. I've moved on, just like I'm sure you moved on with the Web Wench."

"Mallory's moved on with *Go Here Now*, the start-up travel site launched by the guys who founded Twitter. She's leaving us next week and moving to Silicon Valley."

As is probably obvious, I was delighted by this news. "But she's only worked for you for—what—three months?"

"Six. She did a good job, but she jumps around a lot. I'm looking for a web person who'll hang around."

"Well, you're free to hire anyone you want. Not my business anymore. You're also free to show up late for important occasions, buy microwaves, do anything that—"

"The microwave." He sighed. "I could kick myself."

"Be my guest."

"But it wasn't the worst idea. Your old microwave died, and you can't function without one," he said. "I thought you'd appreciate it, I really did,"

"Your 1100-watt, stainless steel Cuisinart with its eight pre-programmed, time-based settings wasn't the reason why I broke up with you."

"My being late was the bigger sin?"

"Do I really need to spell it out for you, Simon? It was because of your months of buildup to what I thought was a proposal that never came. Period. End of story."

"I knew that. I'm nervous because I want us back together, so I'm coming off like a dense jerk right now. Sorry."

"I remain unmoved."

"Doesn't it say something that I drove up here to make things better? Jackie and Pat thought so."

"My friends are pushovers, which, as you know, I am not." I checked my watch. "In the five minutes you have left, tell me why you want us back together and how you think things would be different this time."

Simon took a huge deep breath and several seconds before proclaiming: "I'm ready to make a commitment."

I'm. Ready. To. Make. A. Commitment. That's how he said it—very slowly and with an exaggerated gravitas, as if he were the President of the United States declaring the end of a long, drawn-out conflict with a hostile nation.

"What does that mean?" I asked. "You've said it before."

"It means I don't want us to be apart," he said. "You're my *habibi*."

"Your what?"

"*Habibi*. It's Arabic for 'my beloved.' One of our writers just turned in a piece about King Abdullah of Jordan. The king calls his wife that."

"How nice for her." I couldn't keep my hands still. They were on my knees. They were in my hair. They were massaging the back of my neck. Why couldn't he just say it, for Christ's sake? What was so hard about spitting out, "Elaine, will you marry me?"

"We could have a schedule," he said. "Instead of just, you know, you coming over to my place one weekend and me coming over to yours another weekend, with nights here and there during the week, we could formalize it more."

"Oh, please. You sound like a divorced father arranging custody of the kids with his ex-wife." Part of me felt sorry for him the way he was struggling. The other part felt like ripping out his larynx.

"Let me try again." He cleared his throat. "I love you. I love your mind. I love your sense of humor. I love your face and your body and your smell. I—"

"You love my smell? Which one?"

"All of them, but especially the one after you've just been to the blow dry place."

"Must be my stylist's vanilla-scented dry shampoo. She uses it at the root to give me more volume."

"I love how you tell me things like that. Most men would hate hearing about the minutiae of a woman's hair appointment, but I don't hate it because it's you."

I have to admit I was rather touched by that and therefore had no snappy comeback.

"Let me cut to the chase," he said. "I just told you I'm almost ready to make a commitment and I meant—"

"*Almost?* You're *almost* ready?" Unbelievable. He was backtracking already.

"Yeah, and the reason I'm stuck at 'almost' is because of the last time I was ready to walk down the aisle."

"So this is about Jillian?"

"She and I would be married right now if I'd been able to save her." His tone was no longer teasing, and his eyes reflected the pain he still felt about the sailing accident that took the life of his fiancée.

"Her death was terribly, terribly tragic," I said softly, "and what happened to you would leave anyone emotionally damaged." He and Jillian had set a date for their wedding. He'd been assigned a story for the magazine on the British Virgin Islands and she'd gone along on the trip—a honeymoon before the wedding. They'd chartered a sailboat, a storm had blown up, and she'd fallen overboard, lost at sea. She was dead and he blamed himself.

"Right, exactly. So give me more time to come around."

"I can't."

"Why not?"

"Self-preservation. I don't know if you'll ever get over her, and you don't know if you'll ever get over her, and truthfully, I don't know if your grief and guilt are the real problem. Either way, it's not fair to keep me in limbo forever."

I got up from the Adirondack chair, which wasn't easy because I had slid back into the curved seat and was sort of trapped there. "It's been ten minutes," I said, weary of his chronic vacillating. "I think you should go back to New York."

"Nope," he said. "I can't take a chance of suddenly realizing I'm ready to move forward and having the realization hit me while I'm in the city instead of here with you. I should stay for the rest of the week just in case I have my aha moment sooner rather than later."

"Your aha moment? What are you, Oprah?" So he was back to being the smart-ass. "I'm sick of the jokes, sick of this whole roller coaster, sick of you. Just go, Simon. Now."

"You're right. Big day tomorrow." He rose from his chair, stretched, and yawned. "Just to be clear, I love you, Slim."

"Good luck with that," I said, went inside and slammed the door behind me.

Day Three:
Wednesday, July 17

8

"Who wants to go first?" asked the heavily bearded Wes, Whitley's head farmer, whose black rubber boots presumably kept him from slipping and sliding in manure.

"I will," said Lake. "I need to feel a kinship with the cow, to be in harmony with her, to let her know how grateful I am for the bounty she provides."

This woman was making me ill. Or was it the fact that I hadn't eaten breakfast? Not that there would have been time. We'd had to get up at an ungodly hour to make it to Whitley's 5:30 a.m. milking. It didn't help my queasiness that the dairy barn, while fastidiously maintained and ventilated, smelled like a giant shit box.

"Come ahead then," said Wes, waving Lake closer. We were all gathered around one of the stalls, observing a very large cow named Missy, who was positioned so that we could view her in all her glory. She was black and white—a Holstein, we were told—and she had affecting brown eyes along with this…this…thing hanging down from underneath her torso. It wasn't exactly a belly, but it was so bloated and saggy it reminded me of mine after eating too much cauliflower. Wes began to massage it with a tenderness I found very appealing. "I'm relaxing Missy's udder so the milk will drop right down to the bottom," he explained. "See her face? She's ready. She's chewing her cud, which tells you it's time."

"Before you start," said Gabriel, his hawkish face contorted with dread, "I'm confirming that the cows here are not—I repeat not—fed some corn-grain mixture, because I wouldn't be okay with that, and neither would my wife. We eat only grass-fed meats, which are lower in calories and contain healthier, omega-3 fats, more vitamins A and E, and higher levels of antioxidants. No antibiotics or hormones in their bodies either, right?"

Wes nodded patiently, as if he'd fielded plenty of similar questions from other city folk who spent too much time at Whole Foods. "Only grass-fed at Whitley," he said, in a delightful "yup" and "nope" monotone I vowed to adopt so as to seem more composed, impervious to life's every irritant. "No need for antibiotics or hormones, because our cows don't get sick. The average lifespan of a cow in America is three to four years. Missy, the gal you'll be milking today, is fourteen."

"She's almost old enough for Medicare," said Simon, Mr. Laugh-a-Minute. I'd told my friends about our ten-minute conversation the previous night and, predictably, they thought I'd been too hard on him, that "almost ready" was pretty damn close to being ready and that I shouldn't write him off.

"You know, some of us depend on Medicare," Beatrice

snapped at Simon. "Particularly if we can't depend on our children in our time of need."

"Oh come on, Mother," Jonathan said with a tolerant smile. "It's okay to take a day off from the harangue."

"You see how he speaks to me?" she said, looking to the rest of us for affirmation. Nobody gave it to her.

"Do cows really have four stomachs?" Jackie asked Wes.

"Yup," he said. "We feed 'em, and then each stomach breaks the food down a little more and a little more. After it gets to the first stomach, they regurgitate it and chew it again."

"Now that's one way to get the most bang for your buck," said Ronnie with a chuckle.

"Could we please get back to milking the cow?" said Lake, who was probably dying to rush into the kitchen to cook with Chef Hill again. I'd noticed the day before that she was absorbing every pearl of his wisdom about food and the planet and the farmer and that she stood next to him at every opportunity with the sort of worshipful look you'd afford the Pope.

"Step on over," Wes invited her. "Crouch down here next to me, and we'll give Missy a run."

Lake kneeled beside Wes. He pointed to the four pink appendages that protruded from Missy's udder. If I tell you the pink appendages looked like penises, you'll remember that I told you the pork tenderloins looked like penises and you'll think I have a penis fetish. I just don't know how else to describe them.

"These are her teats," said Wes. He took Lake's hand. "Wrap your forefinger around first, then the middle finger, then the ring finger, and close them around the teat to seal it. Now squeeze it."

No sooner did she squeeze than milk squirted out. It was a miracle—completely mesmerizing!

"Who's next?" asked Wes. "Once we're done with the show-and-tell, I'll hook Missy up to the pump and tank, and milk her that way. Much faster."

Before I knew what had gotten into me, my hand shot up. Wes beckoned me over. I crouched down beside him, right underneath Missy's udder. Apparently, I crouched down too low, because my hair got tangled in her teats and it took me a minute to extricate myself.

"First the forefinger, then the middle finger, then the ring finger, then close 'em up and squeeze," he coached.

The contact of my fingers around Missy's warm, baby-soft teat was exquisitely satisfying for some reason, and I was enchanted. I squeezed the teat, timidly at first and then more confidently, and when the milk came out, I heard myself sigh with pleasure. It felt so natural, so organic, so… spiritual, as if I were nursing a baby or something. I know, I know. I sound like Lake, but it was very rewarding.

Reluctantly, I stood up and let the next person have their turn. Everybody except Beatrice milked Missy, who was such a good sport that she never kicked, never budged, not even when Simon decided to hum *You Are the Sunshine of My Life* while he milked, the song they'd played over and over on the cruise ship, the song that had become an inside joke with us during the trip and then had become our special song, perversely. I pretended I didn't notice.

As we were all leaving the barn, Pat agreed that the milking experience reminded her of breast-feeding her children while Jackie said it reminded her of giving her ex-husband Peter a hand job because his penis was as tiny as one of Missy's teats. Alex confided that her fiancé preferred blow jobs to hand jobs and that she was becoming quite proficient at them, which might have explained why he was so ready and willing to make a commitment to her and which forced me to consider whether I should have been more proactive with Simon in that regard.

"How often do you do it to your fiancé?" I asked her as the four of us walked over to Whitley's kitchen.

"*Elaine*," Pat groaned with embarrassment.

"Elaine wasn't the one who brought it up," Jackie reminded Pat before turning back to Alex. "So how often do you do it to him?"

"Whenever and wherever he wants me to," Alex said with a naughty smile before trotting off to join the others.

"Why do guys love blow jobs so much?" said Jackie as we Three Blonde Mice linked arms and strolled on. "I can't figure it out. Is it the tongue action?"

Pat blushed furiously, but managed to say, "Bill thinks it's because men don't have to worry about getting the woman pregnant like they do with intercourse."

"Yeah, but the three of us aren't getting pregnant any time soon," Jackie pointed out. "Neither is Alex."

"I think it's because men are lazy," I said. "When they're getting a blow job, they don't have to do any of the work."

"I think it's because they're pervy," said Jackie. "They can sit up and watch during it, and it turns them on even more."

"I wonder if I'm any good at it," I mused. "Simon didn't say I wasn't, but you never know."

"The only thing I know for sure is you can't let your

teeth near a man's penis," said Pat. "It happened once with Bill, and he called me a cheese grater."

Jackie and I looked at each other and burst out laughing. Pat's line was not only a highly personal admission for her but also the perfect segue into our next activity: learning how to make cheese.

9

Chef Hill kicked off the class with an impassioned speech about the necessity of using fresh dairy products in the food we make for our families. As we sat in our folding chairs like well-behaved students, he told us about his farm in Sharon, Connecticut, where his wife cultured butter from the milk from their cows. "She cultures it with our yogurt and a touch of sea salt, so it's light and airy and spreadable," he said between sniffs of his leaky nose. "She's a dream, my wife. She made a blue cheese the other day and it was so good I nearly cried. And her ricotta? Oh, man. Well, you'll be making it today, so you can tell me what a great mouthfeel it has."

Mouthfeel. Please. While his assistants busied themselves gathering the ingredients for us, I noticed that Lake stepped up to the center island to have a word with him.

"I just wanted to tell you I enjoyed our class yesterday, and I'm looking forward to the rest of the week," she said with a look of awe and wonder. "My life partner and I hold you and your values in the highest esteem, and we try to honor them in our own kitchen and lifestyle. You really have changed the way we look at food and we thank you for your contribution to saving the planet." She nodded and then backed away with a slight bow.

Right behind her was Alex. "It's so much fun learning to cook with you," she said to Chef Hill in a silky, melodic voice that matched her flowing locks and wardrobe. She was one of those women who glided, floated, sashayed in their airy skirts and pants and tops and bandanas. I wondered if she was gentle when she blasted away at her patients' plaque, or whether she was one of those rip-you-to-shreds hygienists. I also wondered whether she talked your ear off while you were sitting in that chair, a captive audience, or whether she went about her business silently, dreaming up screenplay ideas. And, of course, I wondered if she'd met her fiancé while she was cleaning his teeth and, if so, whether it was love at first debridement.

The chef looked pleased by Alex's compliment. No, scratch that, he looked pleased by Alex. The self-proclaimed family man's eyes roamed over her body with such a complete lack of subtlety it was embarrassing. "What's your name again, hon?" he asked, having trouble keeping his tongue in his mouth. "I don't remember it, sorry, but I definitely remember *you*."

"It's Alex. Alex Langer," she said, in a more businesslike tone than she'd used initially, perhaps sensing he was coming on to her. "If you have time at the end of the week, I'd like to interview you for a screenplay I'm writing. I'd only need fifteen or twenty minutes, max."

"A screenplay, huh?" he said. "You wanna do a movie about a humble little guy like me?"

"Not about you, no," said Alex. "My story is about a chef like you. I'd just be using you for research."

Ouch. Even my ego would have been bruised. "Well, I'll see what we can set up," he said. "I'll have one of my people get back to you before the week is out."

As she thanked him and turned away, Jonathan, who was sitting next to me, remarked, "She's kind of attractive."

"Alex?" I smirked. "And I thought I was the object of your affection this week."

I was flirting with Jonathan again, and what about it? Yes, Simon was sitting in the row right behind me, but I was a free woman. My slavish devotion to him was officially over. As a matter of fact, the minute he'd left my cottage last night, I'd gone inside and googled Jonathan. I'd found the website for his law firm and read the "About Jonathan Birnbaum" section along with testimonials from clients. I'd even found a food blog he'd been writing—all of which convinced me that he wasn't a serial killer and that I should make every effort to get to know him better.

"You are the object of my affection, Elaine," he assured me with a twinkle in his eye. "Alex is a distant second. No, make that a very distant second."

"Well, in any case, she's engaged, although I don't know when she ever sees her fiancé. He sounds like a busy man."

"Martha, my last ex-wife, is an ER doc at Good Sam Hospital in West Palm Beach. I never saw her either."

"How did you meet her?"

"I brought my mother to the hospital one night after she called my cell—while I was on a date, naturally—and said she was having a heart attack. It turned out to be the General Tso's chicken she'd ordered from our local Chinese place. She doesn't do spicy."

"Then why did she order it?"

"So she had a reason to ruin my evening. Her manipulation backfired when I ended up marrying Martha."

"Sounds like she makes a habit of having medical emergencies that aren't," I said.

"If you're referring to her slip and fall during the foraging lesson, that was a good example. My interest in a woman brings out her less charming side."

"But you were only being friendly to me."

"I was being more than that, Elaine." He smiled mischievously. "Is it okay if I keep it up? I don't want to come on too strong."

"Actually, it's refreshing for a man to be so forthright," I said, having endured a year of Simon's vacillating. "By all means, keep it up."

10

I was stuck with Lake for the cheese making. Each group—Jackie got Jonathan, Pat got Ronnie, Alex got Connie and Beatrice, Gabriel got Simon—was given a large pot of the milk that had just flowed from Missy's teats.

"The milk you're working with is the purest of the pure," said Chef Hill. "Compared to the milk you buy in the supermarket, it's like the difference between a tomato from the garden and a container of ketchup. I want you to taste a teaspoon of it before we begin—just to sample what our planet, if left unspoiled, has to offer us." He actually wiped a tear from his left eye. "Look at me, getting all emotional," he said. "I can't even talk about our planet anymore without choking up."

"Please don't apologize," said Lake. "You're a beautiful person, Chef. You care so passionately."

"Yeah, you're really passionate," said Connie, not to be outdone in the fawning department. She must have forgiven him for yelling at her yesterday. "I was at that food fair in

Seattle when you got emotional about overfishing. 'Every time an Atlantic halibut gets caught in a gillnet, the planet cries,' you told us."

"Your first cookbook is my bible," said Lake.

"Yeah, but *I* have *all* his cookbooks," said Connie, eyeing Lake as if they were bidding against each other at an auction. "And they're *all* my bibles."

"Ladies, the important point is that I believe we should treat the planet with tenderness," said Chef Hill after clearing his throat and mopping his tear-stained face with a dishtowel. "My cooking has always reflected that belief, long before others promoted themselves as farm-to-table know-it-alls. It amazes me how many pretenders there are out there. I see all those ridiculous blogs written by people who claim to be experts about food. I don't take them or their recipes seriously, and neither should you."

I glanced over at Jonathan, hoping he wasn't deflated by the swipe at bloggers, but I could tell by his flared nostrils that he was more than a little annoyed. And who could blame him? Between his mother dissing his interest in being a chef and his cooking teacher dissing his blog, the guy couldn't get any respect.

Chef Hill instructed us again to dip a teaspoon into our pot of milk and taste it.

"Wow, it's still warm," I said, thinking of Missy's teat and wondering if I'd collapse and die (cause of death: non-pasteurization of milk).

"That's why it's called pure," said Lake. "It's from a cow, not a carton." She sighed showily, as if I'd just said the earth was flat. "But don't worry, Elaine. We're all here to learn and grow and absorb, so you'll come to appreciate what the farm-to-table movement is about in time."

I laughed. She was unintentionally funny with her foodie nuttiness. "Thanks for your patience while I learn and grow and absorb," I replied.

"Now, are we all ready to make our ricotta and have a true cow-to-kitchen experience?" asked Chef Hill. "Let's do it. Bang bang."

Lake and I went about our business. She added the tablespoon of citric acid to the pot, and I tossed in the teaspoon of cheese salt. She stirred, and then I stirred, and we were supposed to keep stirring until the heat reached 185 degrees.

"This ricotta recipe, as well as the others that we'll be utilizing today, is included in the Whitley tote bags Rebecca Kissel handed out at your arrival," the chef reminded us.

Ah yes, the tote bag I still hadn't looked through. I made another mental note to hunt it down when I got back to the cottage later. "As soon as the curds and whey separate, take the pot off the heat and let it set for ten minutes," Chef Hill advised as he stopped by our station and had a peek at our milk.

"How will we know when the curds and whey separate?" Jackie asked from across the kitchen. "I don't even know what curds and whey are except from the Little Miss Muffet nursery rhyme."

"The curds will show up when you get close to that 185 degrees," Chef Hill replied. "You'll begin to see little shiny white lumps, sort of like in cottage cheese."

He made it sound as if the milk would get to the desired temperature quickly. No such luck. Cheese making, I discovered, was a slow, tedious, watching-paint-dry process involving stirring and checking the thermometer and stirring and checking the thermometer and waiting for the curds to show up and then waiting some more. But when we did get curds and they did get shiny, it was very exciting. I even called out to Jackie and Pat, "We have curds! Do you have curds?"

"I have curds," Simon called back to me. "I'll show you my curds if you show me yours."

"Time to stick a fork in it," said Chef Hill. "You've got cheese."

"Oh my God," I said after my taste. "It's light and fluffy and sweet—like what you'd buy, only way better."

"Of course it's good. It came right from one of the earth's creatures," said Lake, who lowered her face so close to the pot to scoop the ricotta onto her fork that I was tempted to drown her big lollipop head in it.

Per Chef Hill's instructions, we poured our cheese into a colander, let the curds drain in a cheesecloth, and transferred the ricotta to a large bowl, setting the stage for the real cooking to begin.

11

We used our homemade ricotta in three ways. We stuffed it into zucchini blossoms, lightly fried them, and sprinkled them with fresh thyme leaves and lemon zest. We stuffed it into the fresh tortellini we made and baked them with a zippy tomato sauce. And we stuffed it into the chickens that were the very creatures we'd said hello to that morning on our way to the dairy barn when they were still alive and pecking—chickens that we roasted over a layer of hay moistened with white wine. (Wine or no wine, the hay still smelled like pot.)

"Did you have fun cooking with Ronnie?" I asked Pat as the Three Blonde Mice sat at the dining table with the others, enjoying our meal at the end of what was a long day on our feet. While Jackie was polishing off another glass of Pinot Gris, Pat and I were savoring the peach galette over which Lake and I had nearly come to blows. Yes, I was clumsy rolling out the dough for the galette—I had rolled it so aggressively that it had careened right off the countertop onto the floor and we'd had to start over—but she didn't have to keep flicking me with flour and getting it in my hair. She said she was just kidding around, but being a humorless sort, she didn't know the first thing about kidding around and the end result was that I looked like some eighteenth-century British monarch in a powdered wig. Gabriel saw what had happened, hurried over, and said to me in a low, confessional tone, "She's been under a lot of stress lately," as if that explained her behavior.

"Ronnie had his fingers in everything," said Pat. "We didn't have any ricotta to stuff our chicken with because he ate it all."

"Jonathan told me how much he likes you, by the way," said Jackie.

"Maybe he just wants to get laid," I said.

"Then he should have picked me to like," she cracked. "Did you tell him you're taken?"

"No," I said, "because I'm not."

"*Elaine*," Jackie sighed.

"Simon and I are not a couple." I watched her pour herself another glass of wine and couldn't help myself. "Do you really need to drink so much?"

"It's not 'so much.'" She gave me a "Jackie" look, which involved jutting out her chin. "I'm not an alcoholic. I just like to drink. You need to stop being a cop, Elaine."

I held up my hands in surrender. "I care about you, that's all."

"Yeah, well care a little less," she said, and went right back to her wine. "So are you interested in Jonathan or just trying to make Simon jealous enough to propose?"

"Both," I admitted.

She took another sip of wine. "Speaking of proposing, Alex told me her fiancé proposed at the observation deck at the Empire State Building. The view was great, but when they went through all those metal detectors, one of the inspectors made him empty his pockets and out came the ring. Not very romantic."

"Or original," I said. "The dreaded Eric proposed to me in Times Square on New Year's Eve. He kept getting jostled by the crowd and ended up dropping the ring on the street and not being able to find it. Then a guy in earmuffs and a pointy red party hat picked it up and said he'd give it back for a hundred bucks. Since Eric couldn't find a cop willing to take on such a trivial matter on the city's busiest night of the year, he haggled with the guy while I stood there freezing my ass off, and eventually they settled on fifty dollars. He bitched and moaned about having to shell out more money for the already-expensive ring and in between the bitching and moaning he asked me to marry him. He was a jerk for screwing up the proposal and I was a jerk for saying yes to it."

"Getting back to you and Jonathan," said Jackie, "it's a little weird with Simon here, but you two seem to be hitting it off. You and Jonathan, I mean."

"You do," Pat agreed.

Just then I felt a hand on my shoulder. I spun around in my chair and there was Jonathan. He smiled at my friends but saved his biggest smile for me. "Do you mind if I have a quick word, Elaine?"

Jackie winked at me unsubtly, reached for her wineglass, grabbed Pat with her other hand and led them both toward the other end of the table where Simon was sitting. He was making faces at me—the kind of faces a child makes:

sticking out his tongue, crossing his eyes, pulling on his ears and wiggling them. Very mature.

Jonathan planted himself in Jackie's chair and pulled it closer to mine. He smelled of pastry dough, which made me think of my flour fight with Lake. "Great meal, wasn't it?" he said.

"A little too great," I said, patting my stomach. I was so full I was dying to open the zipper on my jeans.

"The only negative was that I didn't get to cook with you again," he said, draping his arm along the back of my chair in a way that felt proprietary, courtly, as if he were wrapping his arm around my shoulders, around me. He really was good looking, with his intense eyes and aristocratic nose. I liked the way his hair curled around his ears too—short enough to be well-groomed but long enough to announce that he was not just another buttoned-up lawyer.

"So you don't mind that Chef Hill has it in for food bloggers?" I asked. "I googled you and you write one—a blog, I mean. It's impressive, Jonathan. Did you come up with all those recipes yourself?"

"I did, thanks. Chef Hill is crazy if he thinks food bloggers are going away anytime soon. We may not have trained at Michelin-starred restaurants, but we know what we're doing and we're sick of being put down by food snobs like him. One of these days somebody will make him eat his words." He cleared his throat, shifted in his chair. "Sorry to get so wound up. On a more pleasant note, I could order us a couple of cognacs and we could sit on the terrace, sip the brandy, gaze up at the stars, and listen to the goats bleat."

"How do you know what it sounds like when goats bleat?" I teased. "Are there that many of them in Palm Beach?"

"Are you kidding? We have plenty of goats, but ours are special: They play mahjong." He laughed his jolly laugh. "The offer of a terrace rendezvous expires in five minutes."

"I'd like to," I said, "but we got up so early to milk the cows, and I'm dead."

He looked wounded. "I promise not to keep you out late. I won't even regale you with stories about my legal work, as riveting as wills, trusts, and estates are. Come on. Say yes."

He was such a decent man. I would grow to love him in time. We would have one of those long, happy marriages that begin with friendship and blossom into a sexual relationship aided and enhanced by pharmaceuticals. We would be supremely compatible. I would continue to climb the ladder at Pearson & Strulley, commuting to Palm Beach on weekends, and he would continue to draw a healthy income from his law practice with a possible restaurant venture on the side. We'd never have to lose sleep over money. We would travel often and eat well and invite Beatrice to our home on Sundays and holidays until such time as she was ready to relocate to one of those upscale, beautifully appointed memory care facilities. It would be a wonderful, enriched life full of culture and shared values. Jonathan, for example, would never be late for my birthday dinners nor surprise me with microwaves. "Sure. I'll meet you for cognac and goat bleating. Give me ten minutes."

"Great." He looked ecstatic, which was flattering. It was nice to know that the prospect of being in my presence could instill such enthusiasm in an attractive man, a man who was so unafraid of committing to a woman that he'd done it twice.

12

After a quick trip back to my cottage to apply more insect repellent and throw on a long-sleeved top—the bugs came out in force once the sun went down—I met Jonathan in the area of the farm between the dairy barn and the hen house. There were wrought iron chintz-covered chaise lounges on a large stone patio illuminated with tasteful ground lighting and tall citronella torches. Jonathan was stretched out in one of a pair of side-by-side chaises, two brandy glasses set up on a small table next to him.

"Have a seat and sit a spell," he said. "The stars are out, but I haven't heard a single bleat yet. A cow mooing here and there, but no bleats."

"Mooing will do," I said, getting comfortable in the other chaise. He clinked his glass with mine, and we each took a sip. I tried not to make a face. It tasted like kerosene, but there was no point in spoiling the moment.

"What should we talk about?" he said. "I promised not

to drone on about my legal work, but feel free to tell me about your work at Pearson & Strulley."

"I'd rather hear about you, Jonathan. You mentioned that your second wife was a doctor. What did the first one do?"

"Ah, Joni with an *i*." He sighed in a way that suggested she'd been a handful. "She's one of the war stories I mentioned. When I met her, she was a real estate agent with the Sotheby's office in town. She sold me my house, as a matter of fact. After we got married, she stopped showing houses and became passionately interested in polo—or, to be more specific, polo players. I had a miserable sinus infection one winter and left work at about three o'clock to crawl into bed. Unfortunately, it was already occupied: Joni and Marcos, an Argentinian stud from the polo club, were road-testing the mattress. When they saw me standing in the doorway, they grabbed the sheets to cover themselves, just like in the movies, and blurted out, "It's not what it looks like," which made me laugh. Why do people say that? It's always what it looks like. Anyway, I kept my house in the divorce and Joni moved into a condo at the polo club where she's been running through their roster of players ever since."

"I'm so sorry," I said. "I didn't catch my ex and his girlfriend in the act, but being cheated on isn't fun."

"No, but when I look back on both my marriages, I can see that I made poor choices," said Jonathan. "Martha was consumed with her job and didn't really want a personal life, and Joni gave up her job so she could have a personal life that didn't include me. The next time around I wouldn't mind a wife who'll make me more than an afterthought."

"Sounds like a reasonable qualification." I liked that Jonathan was so open about his relationships. Prying information out of Simon about anything was hard work. Jonathan was easy, and I was in the mood for easy.

We talked for another hour or so. He told amusing stories about the snowbirds in Palm Beach. He said what a relief it was when they all flocked north after Easter because he could finally get a table at a decent restaurant, a parking space at the local Publix supermarket, and a respite from the hectic round of parties. I told what I hoped were amusing stories about my clients at Pearson & Strulley and how rewarding it was when I was able to get them media attention for an actual accomplishment instead of trying to put a positive spin on something idiotic or even criminal they'd done. As I said, Jonathan was easy to talk to. I didn't have to strain to make conversation. We commiserated about being only children and how it was a plus not having to deal with sibling rivalry but a minus not being able to deflect parental attention. We had a lot in common, it turned out. Like me, he was part of a trio of friends who got together often. Like me, he preferred companionship but was perfectly fine with living alone. Like me, he placed importance on honesty and trustworthiness. When he walked me back to my cottage, he lingered on the porch, as if contemplating whether to kiss me goodnight. And then he did kiss me goodnight. It was a soulful kiss that became a series of soulful kisses involving lip contact, tongue contact, my arms around his neck and his arms around my waist, even a little below-the-waist exploration.

"You're a terrific woman, Elaine," said Jonathan a bit breathlessly when we broke apart.

I wasn't breathless—it had been a little odd and disorienting to kiss someone other than Simon—but I wasn't a store mannequin, either. Having a man find me desirable triggered a reciprocal desire in me. I liked having Jonathan touch me and said so.

"I'm trying to be a gentleman, since we just met," he said. "But we're two mature adults with no reason not to express our feelings, right?"

"Right."

He kissed me once more, said goodnight, and stepped off my porch into the night.

As I was turning to go inside, standing there fumbling in my bag for my key, pondering my life as Mrs. Birnbaum of New York and Palm Beach, I heard someone clomping onto the porch and assumed Jonathan had been unable to contain himself and come back for more kissing.

"Hello," said Simon, as if he didn't have a care in the world. He might as well have been whistling the way he was standing there with that happy-go-lucky look on his face. "So you were out with what's-his-name?"

"Jonathan, yes," I said. "Were you spying on me?"

"Not exactly. I saw him leave, that's all."

"I like him," I said. "Just so you know."

"Duly noted. Now, how about taking a walk with me?"

"No, Simon."

"Want to stay here and talk?"

"No, Simon."

"Want to sneak into the dairy barn and milk Missy?"

"Okay, that's enough," I said. I'd found my key and opened the door. "I can't prevent you from finishing out the week here, but I think I've been more than straight with you. Call me unreasonable. Call me insensitive. Call me self-protective. It doesn't matter. The bottom line is still this: I don't want any involvement with you unless and until you're all in and maybe not even then."

"None at all?" He stared at me with those stupidly gorgeous baby blues.

"That's correct."

"Not as a friend?"

"I have enough friends. No."

"Not as someone you can tell your deep, dark secrets to?"

"I don't have any deep, dark secrets. Weren't you the one who said I was born without a filter?"

"Right. How about as a lover then? I could ravish you between cooking classes."

"Goodnight, Simon," I said and closed the door behind me.

13

I luxuriated in a warm, soothing bath fortified with Whitley's eucalyptus and vanilla bath salts. The idea was to get clean, of course. I'd spent the morning in a dairy barn, after all, and while Missy the cow was an enchanting creature with whom I would always feel an intimate connection, I did stick my face in her pristine-but-nevertheless-farm-animal privates. But the bath was also to decompress after the long, emotionally complicated day.

After I nearly fell asleep in the tub, such were its restorative powers, I revived, stepped out onto the cool marble floor, and toweled off. Next came Whitley's creamy, rich, lavender-and-jasmine body lotion, which I slathered all over my pruned skin before folding myself into their white velour robe with an elegant shawl collar. If it was possible for a neurotic, tightly coiled New Yorker with boyfriend problems to feel Zen-like and serene, I did at that moment.

It was in this blissful state that I decided it really was time to find Whitley's tote bag with the recipes, Chef Hill's bio and cookbook, and whatever else Rebecca Kissel had stuffed into the bag, so I went searching around the cottage. I looked in the clothes closet. I looked in the coat closet. I looked in the bottom drawer of the dresser. I even looked under the bed, just in case the housekeeper had stowed it there while she was vacuuming.

"There you are," I said when I found the bag in the corner, shoehorned between the chaise and the oversized suitcase I'd crammed with pants and tops and shoes, most of which would have been more appropriate for a week on the French Riviera.

There really wasn't much of interest in the bag, I discovered, as I toted the tote over to the bed, plopped down on the duvet, and dumped the contents in front of me. I had expected free goodies, as in cheeses, chocolates, a bottle of wine—something tempting thrown in with all the press releases and directives—but there was just a bunch of papers along with the cookbook.

"No swag here," I said. I made piles of the tote bag's contents on the bed: a pile for Chef Hill's information, a pile for the recipes, and a pile for miscellany—i.e. the history of Whitley Farm, a site map of the property, testimonials from past travelers, a FAQ sheet, the schedule for our agritourism week, and a list of activities for the Saturday Bounty Fest finale.

I was about to toss the last document into the miscellany pile—I figured it was just Rebecca welcoming us yet again to our week of fun and games—when my eyes lit on the letter's addressee. Instead of *Dear Cultivate Our Bounty Guests*, *Dear Agritourists*, or *Dear Farm-to-Table Enthusiasts*, the letter read: *Dear Pudding*.

Who in the world was Pudding?

Because of my advancing age, I held the letter at a distance so I could actually see its words without squinting.

"What are you all about?" I asked the letter, and started reading.

There was something in there about a cooking video on YouTube. There was something in there about the chef in the video loving pudding. There was something in there about Hollywood movies in which villains dissolved and vaporized—a lot of drivel is what I'm saying, and I was surprised. Rebecca had struck me as a levelheaded, high-minded sort of woman, but judging by the letter she wrote to "Pudding," she must have had a silly, whimsical side too.

I was about to keep going, keep reading, but then I stopped. Abruptly. It was the first sentence of the second paragraph that seized me with a sense of foreboding and caused my throat to constrict.

The letter wasn't from Rebecca at all, it turned out, but rather from a member of my group, someone I'd foraged with and milked with and made cheese with, and the recipient was…. Well, the letter must have been intended for Chef Jason Hill, even though I'd been the recipient instead. Why I was the recipient, I couldn't fathom.

I signed up to be a guest at the hotel's Cultivate Our Bounty week just so I could get close to you, but since we won't have quality time alone until the very end, I thought I should write a quick note to say how much I despise you.

Sheesh. Somebody sure didn't like Chef Hill. He wasn't my favorite person either and, as I've said, I planned to critique his teaching style on various websites, but it wouldn't occur to me to write a letter trashing him to his face.

Yes, despise you. Does it scare you to hear that? Are you shocked that someone doesn't think you're God's greatest gift to the world? I'll pretend to be your fan for the entire week, and you'll probably buy my act, because you don't have a clue. You walk around like you're this important chef, someone whose passion in the kitchen we're supposed to admire, but we both know you're in it for the money and the ego. You're all about having foodies slobber over you as a promoter of the farm-to-table movement—excuse me, the farm-to-fork movement. Or is it plough-to-plate, cow-to-kitchen, barn-to-bistro, or mulch-to-meal? I can't keep track of your terminology anymore, can you? Bottom line: There's only one movement you promote, and it's your own.

I started to hyperventilate. It wasn't that I didn't agree that Chef Hill was a phony or that the farm-to-table thing had gone beyond the bounds of sanity, but the writer's tone was angry, threatening, and personal, and it made me very anxious—so anxious that I tried doing a mindfulness meditation involving a warm sandy beach. I tried imagining healing energy in the form of shimmering golden light traveling through my crown chakra right down to the tips of my toes. And I tried Andrew Weil's 4-7-8 breathing exercise, which required me to purse my lips and make *whoosh* sounds.

Nothing worked. I set the letter on the bed very gingerly, as if it might detonate, and reached into the drawer of the night table, rummaged frantically among my antacids, fiber supplements, and hand sanitizers, located the Xanax, and popped one.

I allowed my heart rate a few minutes to return to near normal and read the rest of the letter, knowing full well that my week at Whitley had most likely taken a dark and possibly devastating detour.

You're a fraud—100 percent con artist. You wouldn't know authenticity if it hit you over the head with one of your overpriced cast iron skillets. You have the image of this do-gooder who's all about the land and the farmer and the planet, when in fact you have no conscience, no remorse for your actions. Do you know how much those actions enrage me? Enrage me, as in pure, unprocessed, non-genetically modified rage. If you don't get that, you will—as soon as it sinks in that your miserable life is nearly over. When that happens, your instinct will be to use this letter to protect yourself, but you won't show it to anybody: not the police, not even the little toads who work for you, because you have too many secrets of your own and can't risk the exposure. Pretty interesting predicament you're in, wouldn't you say?

Yes, whatever was eating the writer was personal, deeply felt, and dangerous. Chef Hill needed protection from this person—that much was obvious—and I planned to alert him and his entourage so they could determine who was harboring a massive grudge against him. Surely whatever skeletons were in the chef's closet wouldn't prevent him from trying to root out the loony tune in our midst and hand him or her over to law enforcement right away. In all probability, the letter writer was simply venting—didn't we all need to blow off steam from time to time? This didn't mean the writer actually intended to cause bodily harm. It calmed me down to believe that. But then I had to finish reading the damn letter, of course I did, and there was nothing and no one that could calm me down by the time I got to the end.

I'm sorry about having to kill you on Saturday at the Bounty Fest thing. Not because you deserve to live—we're all better off with you dead, believe me—but because killing isn't something I do on a regular basis, and I really don't want to get caught. There's always the chance that some unlucky bastards could show up in the wrong place at the wrong time, and I'd have to take them out too. Still, while I'd rather not commit multiple murders, killing you will be so satisfying after what you did that I'll just have to shrug off potential collateral damage. Besides, any idiots who fall for your Cultivate Our Bounty bullshit deserve whatever they get.

I was a mess after reading that, Xanax or no Xanax. The saliva in my mouth dried up even as my skin grew cold and slick. I was exploding with questions, so many questions, and in the dead quiet of my cottage with only the occasional cricket chirps for company, I couldn't begin to answer them.

My initial ones were these:

Which of my fellow agritourists wrote the letter?

Which of my fellow agritourists was a good enough actor to pretend to care about agritourism?

What incident or series of incidents between one of my fellow agritourists and Chef Hill had provoked the letter?

How did the letter find its way into my tote bag given that all the tote bags were lined up on the hospitality table during the Happy Hour Welcome Party, each with our name tag on them?

Why couldn't Jackie and Pat and I take a simple vacation together without somebody trying to kill somebody, for God's sake, and what the hell was I supposed to do about it?

14

I slipped the letter into the pocket of my Whitley robe, put on my socks and sneakers, and hightailed it over to Pat's cottage, where we'd agreed to meet after I'd called both my friends and told them I had an urgent matter to discuss.

Praying I wouldn't get caught running around outside in my robe, I ran into Lake and Gabriel, who were taking their nightly walk around the grounds.

"Exercising after a meal is the key to good bowel health," he said.

"Absolutely," I said, nodding vigorously. "That's why I'm out here. Much better than Dulcolax."

"You shouldn't take laxatives," Lake scolded. "They're loaded with chemicals, and your colon becomes dependent on them."

I held my hands up in surrender. "Never again." I was dying to get away from this crazy couple even as I was regarding them intently. Could one of them have written the letter to Chef Hill? Did he, too, take nightly constitutionals, and had there been an argument of some sort while all three of them were tending to their bowel health? And then I remembered that the letter was written before the start of Cultivate Our Bounty week, so the would-be killer must have had a pre-agritourist grudge.

"See you tomorrow," I said to the VanderKloot-Arnolds, and beat it.

Pat and Jackie were waiting by the door when I got there, and they both smelled of alcohol. Apparently, Jackie and Alex had gotten chummy and made a routine of going to Whitley's bar for a nightcap or two, and Pat had joined them this once, sipping an iced chocolate Bailey's Irish Cream concoction with a straw instead of throwing back margaritas like they did. The result was that I had gone to my friends about a life-and-death situation, and they were not at full mental capacity.

"Uh-oh," said Jackie when I showed up. "It's the booze police."

"I just want to talk," I said, "and not about that."

Jackie was teetering as she plunked herself down on Pat's bed. She was slurring her words too. I was determined to keep my mouth shut about her drinking during the trip, but once we were home, I was letting her have it. As for Pat, she was tipsy, and stumbled and nearly fell as she made her way over to the chair.

"What's so terrible that you had to drag us away from the bar?" Jackie asked as I faced them both. "You look pale. Are you sick or something?"

"This is not about my health," I said. "It's about Chef Hill's."

Jackie stared at me. "You're kidding, right? I mean, not that I wish the guy any harm, but who cares?"

"Someone is planning to kill him—someone in our agritourism group," I said, and waited for them to boo and hiss and call me a paranoid neurotic.

"*Elaine.*" Jackie shook her head at me and groaned on cue. "I love you, honey, but you're a psycho sometimes. Jeez. I was enjoying my drink, and you had to get me over here for some bullshit plot of yours? Give it a rest. We're on vacation."

"She can't help it, Jackie," said Pat, who didn't like anybody to be mean. "She worries. Some people are worriers, that's all."

I pulled the letter out of my pocket. "You'll understand after you read this. It was in my Whitley tote bag. It's a death threat."

"*Elaine,*" Jackie groaned again. "It's probably a prank cooked up by Rebecca's staff because life can't be that exciting for kids working on a farm in the summer."

"Like with all that cyber-bullying on Facebook and Twitter," said Pat, "only a letter instead."

"You can trace a tweet and a Facebook post," I said. "The writer of the letter didn't want it to be traced. And by the way, even kids who work on a farm in the summer aren't dumb enough to risk generating bad PR for their employer. No, we're definitely dealing with a real murder plot here."

"You and your murderers," said Jackie.

"Fine. You don't believe me? Here," I said, handing her the letter.

"I don't want it," she said. "I'm too fucking tired."

"Shut up and read it, Jackie," I said. "Out loud so Pat can hear it, unless you're both too impaired."

She gave me the finger and started reading. "Dear Pudding? So it's a recipe?"

"Keep going," I said.

She read, her eyes growing wider with every word, her voice getting quieter and more disbelieving. When she reached the last paragraph about killing Chef Hill and the "unlucky bastards" who might be killed along with him, she let the letter float to the floor and slumped backwards onto the bed, legs splayed. "Not again. Not after last year."

Pat tiptoed over and picked up the letter with the tips of her thumb and forefinger, as if the piece of paper was on fire and she didn't want to get burned. She sat back down and read it silently except for the occasional gasp.

"It was in your tote bag, Elaine?" Jackie finally said, propping herself up.

I nodded. "Obviously it was supposed to go in Chef's Hill's bag, but the letter writer must have been in a hurry and stuck it in mine by accident. I only got around to looking in the bag a little while ago."

Pat came over and hugged me. Then she looked up at me. "What does it all mean?"

"It means that one of our classmates has it in for the chef," I said. "And if we don't act fast, Whitley's Bounty Fest on Saturday will be a crime scene."

She shuddered, went back to her chair, and curled her feet under her, wrapping her arms around her knees. "I can't imagine which of them would do a thing like that. Can either of you? Should I call Bill?"

"Nobody has a tummy ache, so we don't need a

gastroenterologist," Jackie snapped, and immediately apologized. Pat said dumb things occasionally, but getting angry with her was like getting angry at cotton candy.

"We need to take the letter to the police," I said. "Like now."

"But the letter says not to," Pat pointed out. "Maybe it wouldn't be in the chef's best interests to go to anybody."

"It's in the chef's best interests to live past Saturday," I said.

15

We decided to go to Chef Hill first and let him make the judgment whether or not to show the letter to the cops. It was nearly ten o'clock, a little late for paying social calls on famous chefs, but after I ran back to my cottage to change out of my bathrobe, the three of us went to the front desk and asked the clerk for Chef Hill's cottage number.

"I'm sorry," said the clerk, who was chinless and had prominent veins on his nose. "I can't give out the private information of our artisans in residence."

"We're not stalkers or anything." I laughed as if the notion were unthinkable. And then I went right for the bullshit. "His wife is a dear friend of ours, and she asked us to look in on him tonight. She's worried about his health. She said he's been working too hard and not sleeping well."

"If you're such dear friends with Mrs. Hill, why didn't she give you the number of his cottage?" said the clerk.

"She forgot," said Jackie, who made the clerk flinch from her alcohol breath. "And now she's out of cell phone range. We just tried to call her. We tried to call Chef Hill too, but he's not picking up."

"Again, I'm afraid I can't help," he said, turning away from us to focus entirely on the hotel computer screen.

"My husband's a doctor in Manhattan," said Pat. "His name is William Kovecky and he's on *Good Morning America*. He's Chef Hill's personal physician. I'm not at liberty to discuss the chef's condition with you because of the HIPPA law, but my husband felt it was imperative that we see him this evening. This is a potential *medical emergency, sir*."

Wow. Pat was on fire. I'd never seen her so pushy, never mind articulate. The Bailey's Irish Cream must have emboldened her.

When the clerk appeared to be considering his options, she whipped out her driver's license for identification and piped up with, "Google him if you don't believe me: Dr. William Kovecky. He'll be right there on the GMA website. He just did a story for them on Ebola and its gastroenterological symptoms. Did you know that Chef Hill traveled to Africa recently?"

The clerk blanched. "Are you saying what I think you're saying?"

"No, Chef Hill doesn't have Ebola," said Pat as Jackie and I stood back and watched her work, marveling at her chutzpah. "My husband thinks he may have contracted another virus though."

"What she's saying is that you really don't want a famous chef getting sick at your hotel for lack of proper care," I said. "Got it, buddy?"

"Yes, yes, fine, all right," said the clerk, who pulled up the cottage number, wrote it down on a Whitley business card, and handed it to Pat. "Please give Chef Hill my best wishes for a speedy recovery."

I herded my friends out of the lobby—they were unsteady on their feet, to put it mildly—and we made our way to Chef Hill's cottage, which was three times the size of any of ours. When we knocked on the door, we expected one of the minions to answer, but it was Jason himself who greeted us, wearing his fluffy white Whitley robe. With his shaved head and goatee, tattooed neck, and stocky body, he looked like a prizefighter about to get into the ring.

"I didn't know Girl Scouts went door to door at this time of night," he said.

"We're in your cooking class," I said. "I'm Elaine, the one who dropped her galette dough on the floor."

"I remember," he said. "Vaguely."

Jackie and Pat introduced themselves, and we all just stood there for a beat, the way you would if you were up close and personal with a celebrity in his bathrobe. "We hate to bother you, Chef," I said finally, "but we came across something that needs your immediate attention."

"What kind of something?" he asked with a smirk, as if he thought we were groupies jonesing for an autograph.

"A death threat," said Jackie, not bothering to sugarcoat it. She was still slurring her words, and I worried that he wouldn't take her seriously, take any of us seriously. "I think we should come in, don't you?"

The interior of his cottage was a showplace—beamed ceilinged great room, adjoining kitchen and dining room, lovely fixtures and artwork. Only the best for the artisan in residence.

He didn't invite us to sit, so we lingered in his entryway,

where I handed him the letter. "It was put in my tote bag by mistake at the Welcome Happy Hour," I said. "I only got around to reading it tonight."

The three of us watched him read the letter. He was one of those people who moved his lips while he read to himself. When he was finished, he gave the letter back to me as if it were a promotional circular he couldn't wait to throw into the recycling bin.

"Okay, so this is about one of two things," he said. "One: you wrote this because it gave you an excuse to come and see me. I get that you've been partying and maybe hoping for more one-on-one time with me. Happens a lot."

"Oh yeah? What's number two?" I said, not appreciating his attitude. We had come to save his life, and he was treating us like bimbos.

"Two is some nut job guest at the hotel wrote this," he said. "Goes with the territory when you're famous. You wouldn't believe the mail I get accusing me of the most God-awful shit. They threaten to cut off my balls. They say they're gonna kidnap my wife and kids. They compare me to Hitler because I tell people to eat healthy. You grow a thick skin after a while and learn not to give it any oxygen."

"But what if the person who wrote this means it?" said Jackie.

He patted her on the head like you would a good doggie. "I appreciate the thought, but I'm used to this stuff, honest. I just roll with it."

"So you're not even hiring extra security for Saturday?" I said. "A couple of bodyguards wouldn't be a bad idea."

"Nah." He waved me off. "If I put extra security guards

on my payroll every time some wacko said something stupid about me, I'd be broke by now."

He moved us toward the door like a cowboy steering cattle. We protested, tried again to get through to him, but before we knew it we were on his porch in the fetid summer night's air, back to square one.

"Well, that went well," said Jackie. "He totally fucking blew us off."

"What should we do?" said Pat after a loud yawn. As I've said, she wasn't much of a drinker, so she was probably minutes away from passing out.

"We could try Rebecca," I said. "I know where her cottage is. I saw her leaving one morning."

Jackie and Pat were on board, so we hurried—well, I hurried while they lagged—over to see Whitley's executive director. Surely she would put a stop to any bad behavior.

I knocked on her door. No answer. We gave it a minute and tried again. And then I figured what the hell, and turned the doorknob, and we were in. I remembered what Rebecca had told us at the Happy Hour Welcome Party—that Whitley was such a safe, secure environment that some of the staff didn't use their keys and simply left their doors unlocked. I'd snickered when she'd said that, because my apartment in the city had three Medeco locks and a deadbolt and they never went unused.

"Now what?" Pat whispered as we crept into the cottage, which was more of a full-sized cabin where someone would actually live on a full-time basis.

"It's pitch dark in here," said Jackie. "Rebecca must have gone out."

We stood in her entrance hall, trying to get our bearings. "Or she could be asleep," I said.

"Right. It's late, and she probably gets up with the chickens," said Jackie.

"Wait." I put my fingers to my lips to silence my friends. "I think I heard something."

"You always think you hear something," Jackie said.

The dreaded Eric, my ex-husband, used to say I could hear a bird shit in Estonia, and he was right. My hearing was freakishly good. "No, it was sort of a growl. Maybe Rebecca has a pet."

I tiptoed further into the cottage, and when I rounded the corner, into the living room, I stopped in my tracks. Rebecca, it turned out, had not gone out. She wasn't asleep either, nor did she have a pet. She was straddling a naked, bearded man, riding him as if he were one of those mechanical bulls, and she was wearing nothing but a black leather dog collar. Pat let an "Oh!" escape her mouth, and Rebecca looked up to find us gaping at her.

"Who are you and what are you doing in my cottage?" she shrieked, climbing off the man, grabbing a nearby rag rug and wrapping herself in it.

I explained that we were Cultivate Our Bounty guests, and apologized profusely for interrupting.

"Couldn't it wait until tomorrow?" she demanded. She looked mortified.

Her companion, on the other hand, wasn't the least bit uncomfortable. He waved to us from the floor, his privates in full view. "Hey there," he said. "The name's Wes."

"You're the farmer who taught me how to milk Missy,"

I said, recognizing his name and his voice and trying not to look anywhere but above his head.

"You bet," he said in that laconic way he had. It occurred to me that he might very well be a good lover, since he was so familiar with Missy's anatomy. Females were females, when you got right down to it.

"Please don't mention this to anyone," Rebecca begged us. "Wes's wife is our lovely bookkeeper at Whitley. I wouldn't want to hurt her, you understand?"

"But you're sleeping with her husband," I said, not a fan of cheaters, given my histories with my cheating ex and cheating father. "You're already hurting her."

"Elaine, this probably isn't the time for a lecture," said Jackie. "Shouldn't we tell Rebecca the reason we came?"

"Right." I pulled out the letter and started to explain to a woman whose sexcapades had just been cut short about the possible threat to Chef Hill.

"What you're insinuating is impossible," said Rebecca, shuffling toward the front door, her movements hampered by the rag rug she had wound so tightly around her naked body that it caused her to take tiny Geisha steps. "Whitley Farm has an impeccable reputation, and there's never been a scintilla of scandal here."

I almost laughed. No scandal, except that the agritourism director was playing Churn the Butter with the married milker-in-chief. "Why don't we discuss this in your office first thing tomorrow morning?" I suggested.

"There's nothing to discuss," she insisted. "Our guests revere the artisans in residence, including Chef Hill."

"One of them doesn't, according to this letter," I said, waving it at her.

She stared at me, incredulous. "Have you not noticed that Whitley is an idyllic place, a sanctuary where people come to experience the land and its bounty? The philosophy here has to do with harvesting, growing, and sustaining, not killing."

"Some sanctuary," Jackie muttered. "You need a reality check, honey."

Rebecca did not respond, except to close the door in our faces and then turn off the outside light, leaving us in the dark.

"Why was she wearing a dog collar?" asked Pat, feeling around for me so she wouldn't topple over.

"She was dominating," Jackie said. "Or maybe he was dominating. I don't really know."

"Let's table that conversation for now," I said. "We need to go to the police. No way around it."

Jackie belched, polluting the air with her tequila breath, and said, "You drive, Elaine. Pat and I need to rest our eyes."

Fifteen minutes later, we arrived at the Western District of the Connecticut State Police Station. There were two troopers there and they could have made any police department's Best Dressed List. Their shirts were light gray, with royal blue epaulets that matched the royal blue strip down the legs of their navy pants. Their badges were gold, as were their various patches and pins—very four-star general—but it was their hats I liked the most. They were gray Stetsons of the type worn by cowboys, Royal Canadian Mounties, and actors on the old TV show *F Troop*.

"How can we help you, ladies?" asked the one who had introduced himself as Trooper Conway. He had an impressively deep dimple in his right cheek, or perhaps it was an old bullet wound.

"We'd like to report a murder," said Jackie.

"A murder that hasn't happened yet," Pat added.

"It's happening on Saturday," said Jackie. "At Whitley Farm. We're agritourists there."

"We're cultivating our bounty," said Pat. "We milked a cow."

I had decided to let my friends do the talking, since they were always accusing me of trying to control every situation. But from the look on Trooper Conway's face I could see I made a mistake. Pat's brilliance with the hotel desk clerk had given way to fatigue, and Jackie was still in alcohol-ville.

"Have you ladies been drinking?" he asked.

Jackie started to get defensive, but I shushed her. You don't get smart-alecky with a guy who's carrying a semi-automatic pistol, not to mention a baton and pepper spray. "Just a couple of after-dinner drinks," she said, neglecting to mention the numerous glasses of wine she'd consumed first.

"I only had two chocolate milks," said Pat. "Well, it tasted like chocolate milk."

"I'll need to see your driver's licenses, all three of you," said Trooper Conway.

We produced them and waited while the other trooper ran a check on them or whatever it is police officers do with driver's licenses. I got a traffic ticket once, back when I was young and carefree (okay, I was never carefree), and after staring at my license mug shot for what seemed like five minutes the officer handed it back to me and said, "You looked better with bangs." Everyone's a critic.

"I'll need breathalyzer tests," said Trooper Conway after

it was determined that none of us were convicted felons or on Homeland Security's Terrorist Watch List. "Step over here, please."

"Over here" was in the corner of the small barracks, where the officer administered the tests. Basically he told us to take a deep, deep breath and then blow into the little contraption until we couldn't blow anymore. The gizmo calculated the readings and—surprise—Jackie and Pat were over the legal limit.

"You're at .131," he said to Pat. "Point zero-eight is the legal limit."

Jackie was at .151.

"They weren't driving. I was," I said, "so since my test was clean, there's no problem, right?"

"Right," said Trooper Conway, "but all that murder stuff they were talking about is just the alcohol—nothing I can take seriously."

I gave him the letter addressed to "Pudding" and hoped it would change his mind. "There's a plot to kill Chef Hill on Saturday," I said. "That's pretty serious, isn't it?"

He gave it back to me after only a cursory reading. "You city people sure are interesting," he said with an amused shrug. "Which one of you wrote this while you were at the bar having yourselves a good time?"

"We didn't write it!" Jackie protested. "Elaine found it in her tote bag!"

"And I found a million bucks in my wallet," he said. "Look, we've had a lot of experience with the guests at Whitley. You people pay big bucks to come to the boonies so you can pretend to be farmers, and you get bored within twenty-four hours, which leads to all sorts of fun and games. If you ask me, you should go to a casino instead."

"You think we're gamblers?" said Pat, which was not the point.

"What I think is you ladies should go back to the hotel and sleep it off," he said. "It'll be all better in the morning."

He opened the front door and motioned for us to make our exit. Yes, we tried again and again to be heard, but even after I made a rather persuasive case for how I'd discovered the letter and how celebrity chefs got on a lot of people's nerves these days, we were sent on our way.

"We'll have to figure all this out by ourselves," I said as I drove the three of us back to Whitley. "So you two need to sober up. No more nightcaps at the bar. We need to solve this before it's too late. Okay?"

No answer. Nothing. As soon as I stopped at a light, I glanced over at Jackie in the passenger seat and at Pat in the back. They were both fast asleep, their mouths hanging open wide enough to catch flies, as my mother would say.

Day Four:
Thursday, July 18

16

Jackie appeared at my cottage door at 7:00 a.m. Her short, spiky hair seemed to have wilted, and her complexion, usually so ruddy and vivid, was sallow, accentuated by the dark circles under her eyes. If she'd slept at all after I dropped her and Pat off in Whitley's parking lot, it wasn't a restful sleep by the look of her.

Not that I'd logged in more than a couple of hours myself. My brain was flooded with questions about my fellow agritourists and their possible motives for wanting Chef Hill dead. My gut was roiling from nerves, and I'd spent most of the night popping Pepcids.

I motioned Jackie inside and crawled back into bed while she paced back and forth in front of me, back and forth, without saying a word.

"You're making me dizzy," I said.

She stopped pacing. "Just so you know, I'm embarrassed about last night."

"Which part?" I said. "Failing a breathalyzer test or failing me?"

She gave me such a sad face that I quit playing the martyr. I patted the end of the bed. "Come sit. Please."

She did, and I reached out for her hand and held it tightly. "Jackie, listen to me. I love you. And I get what you've been going through this past year. I'd be a disaster if my ex had hired a hit man to kill me on a damn cruise ship. I would have hired a hit man myself—not to kill Eric, just to castrate him."

"You still could," she said with the faintest hint of a smile.

"What I'm saying is you've been drinking more since the cruise, and it's created a distance between us. There have been so many times when I suggest that we do things together, but you always opt for an activity involving a bar and a bottle. Take this trip. Instead of being with Pat and me after our classes at the end of the day, you're with Alex having nightcaps. I'm sure Pat was only at the bar with you last night because she didn't know any other way to get your attention."

"I figured you'd be with Simon every night," she said. "That was the idea when he asked us if he could come."

"Even if he and I were still a couple, which we're not, he loves hanging out with you and Pat," I reminded her. "No excuse there. Sorry."

Silence.

"I'm not the booze police," I went on. "I'm the last one to judge anybody else. I just want you back, Jackie. Drink or don't drink. Up to you. Just don't lose yourself in it."

She nodded. "I didn't even realize that's what I've been doing until last night."

"I need you," I said. "You're my wise, tell-it-like-it-is sounding board, never letting me off the hook but always there when I need you. And now Chef Hill needs you, needs us. Personally, I don't give a shit about him, but we can't let him die."

"No, we can't," she said with her old gusto.

"And since he and the cops don't want anything to do with the death threat, it's up to the Three Blonde Mice to save the day. I have no idea how we're supposed to do that, but are you willing to try?"

She gave me the thumbs-up. "I'm in—100 percent."

Just then Pat arrived. She too did a mea culpa for last night, only she called it a mea gulpa.

"Has anyone noticed that I've been acting like a child?" she said. "That I've regressed into this dim bulb who just goes along and doesn't say what she really thinks and bores everyone with constant references to Bill? How can you stand me?"

"Oh, sweetie. Stop beating yourself up," I said, even though she was right. She'd definitely been acting dim bulbish this week.

"It's like I'm not a mother without the kids around," she said, "and it shocks me how liberating it feels—liberating and scary. I should be missing them more and instead I'm having a great time. My therapist would say I'm acting like a kid to compensate for my guilt."

Pat's therapist, Dr. Margaret Danziger, had written a bestselling book called *Smiley Face* about how to be happy.

Dr. Danziger was currently in the throes of a bitter divorce from a *60 Minutes* producer.

"I think that's very self-aware of you, Pat," said Jackie.

"I agree," I said.

In the end, we aired grievances, admitted fault for various transgressions, vowed to be sturdier, more forgiving human beings. Sometimes friendships need a kick in the ass to keep them on track, and ours was no different. By the time we had to stop schmoozing and get ready for class, the Three Blonde Mice were solid. And we'd come up with phase one of a plan to catch the letter writer—a place to start, anyway.

17

"I like fish. I just don't like the smell, especially this early in the morning," said Jackie. Our group gathered around one of the many seafood counters at the emporium-sized Wendell Brothers Fish Market, a Connecticut institution where every conceivable species of fish and shellfish was sold and distributed to restaurants as well as to the general public. You name it, they had it, fresh or frozen, local or flown in from around the world, resting on a bed of ice in front of us or stored in the back.

"I hear you on the smell," said Alex. She held her nose, which, I noticed for the first time, was unnaturally turned up at the tip in the manner of someone who'd had over-zealous rhinoplasty. "Today is dock-to-dish day, so we'll probably grow gills."

"I like fish, but I don't cook it much at home," said Pat. "The kids will only eat tuna out of a can, and even then it has to have melted cheese on it."

"Do you have any idea how much sodium there is in

canned products?" said Gabriel. "And then there's the mercury." He hovered over Pat to get a better look at the rows of swordfish in the case; they were lined up in perfect symmetry, like synchronized swimmers on Propofol.

"I grew up on canned tuna, Gabriel, and I'm still breathing," said Jackie.

"For now," he said. "But we know so much more about health and wellness than we did all those years ago when you and your friends were growing up."

Jackie snickered. "Way, way back before the invention of the light bulb, you mean?"

While Gabriel's clenched jaw suggested he didn't enjoy being teased, Alex gave Jackie a hug and then headed to another counter to inspect more fish. The two of them really had become fast friends, with Alex promising to fix Jackie up with her fiancé's brother and Jackie promising to landscape the fiancé's patio. But now that Alex was a suspect, Jackie would use their friendship to do some serious probing. We'd decided to probe them all, ask a lot of questions, get a better sense of who had an ax to grind against Chef Hill.

"I don't mean to be impolite, Gabriel," said the always-polite Pat, "but you keep telling others what they should and shouldn't eat and it's getting monogamous."

The malapropism sent Gabriel marching off with a look of superiority. She leaned over and whispered, "Do you think he could be the letter writer?"

"Maybe, but the idea is to engage him in conversation, not alienate him," I said to both my friends.

As far as I was concerned, every member of our group could be the letter writer: Gabriel, Lake, Ronnie, Connie, Alex, Beatrice and, yes, Jonathan. I desperately wanted him not to be the bad guy. Not when our romance was showing such promise. But I couldn't rule him out just because he was a good kisser.

"I think we should tell Simon what's going on and ask him to help," said Pat, who stood on her toes so she could reach up to finger-comb a stray hair out of my face in that gentle, maternal way she had. Since she was short and I was tall, we often had to contort ourselves to make physical contact.

"Good idea," said Jackie.

I glanced over at him as he chatted with one of the fishmongers, and I felt the old pull, the old yearning. It had been Simon who'd helped me bring down the hit man the year before on the ship. Simon who'd taken my ravings seriously. Simon who'd been with me every step of the way until the villain was finally hauled off by the cops. Part of me was dying to tell him there was another nutcase on the loose. The other part wondered how I could confide in a guy who kept disappointing me. "I'll think about it," I said. "But let's get back to the others. Give us a quick snapshot of Alex, Jackie. You've gotten to know her."

"Not that well," she said. "Mostly I pump her for info about her fiancé's single brother. He sounds like a good guy."

"The fiancé or his brother?"

"Both, although I get the feeling that she's settling with her fiancé. She doesn't sound madly in love with him."

"Does this fiancé have a name?" I asked.

"Rick," said Jackie. "If she told me his last name I don't remember it. He runs a successful family business, works all the time, and gives her a sense of security. When she marries him, she'll be able to quit her job and write full time. I think that's the attraction, to be honest."

"Maybe she has a lover on the side," Pat speculated.

"Hm. Like Chef Hill," I said. Maybe the blow-job-proficient Alex Langer was angry that the chef wouldn't leave his wife for her and risk ruining his family-man image. "Has she nailed down her interview with him for her screenplay research?"

Jackie didn't get the opportunity to answer, because Chef Hill himself appeared at the entrance to the market.

"Who wants to get fishy with me today?" he said as he clapped his hands numerous times.

"I do!" Connie's arm shot in the air—both arms, to be precise—and she hooted and cheered and spun around in a happy dance. Then she turned to us and confided, "That's what Chef Hill says whenever he's about to cook fish: 'Who wants to get fishy with me.' I've seen him three times and he always, always says it." To prove that she was a genuine aficionado of his and had come to today's class prepared, she was wearing his nautical blue "Who wants to get fishy with me" T-shirt over her muffin top. Was Connie Gumpers such a fan of his that one cross word from him could send her over the edge? Had he slighted her at a past appearance and she had come to Whitley to prevent him from ever hurting her again?

"Who else wants to get fishy with me?" Chef Hill urged us, clapping his hands again, only this time while he crouched into a squat like a football player about to tackle an opponent. "Come on, people. Let's see some enthusiasm!"

Jonathan edged his way over to me and whispered that he wouldn't mind kissing me right in front of everyone.

I said I wouldn't mind either. I had to pretend nothing was amiss and that we were still on track to become Mr. and Mrs. Birnbaum in order to find out more about him and his true feelings about the chef.

"Jason Hill is an entertaining piece of work, isn't he?" he asked, bumping me lightly with his shoulder. He seemed to want to touch me but was being circumspect in the public setting.

"At least he's trying to educate us about food," I said. I was feeling more compassionate toward the chef since he only had days to live.

"Yeah, he's all about saving the planet through responsible farming and cooking, but, according to an article about him in the *Wall Street Journal*, he's got three mansions, a Gulfstream, a hundred-foot yacht, and a garage full of Ferraris. Not so great for our carbon footprint. Methinks he's not the purist he appears."

There was an undercurrent of bitterness in Jonathan's words. Was he deeply miffed about the chef's swipe at food bloggers—miffed enough to kill him?

"He must make millions from his Planetary Empire operation," I remarked.

"Many millions," said Jonathan. "Makes you wonder if he deserves all the glory he gets."

"You don't think he does?" I said, trying to sound like a merely curious person as opposed to someone who was dying to inject Jonathan with truth serum.

He laughed at himself. "I'm not usually so cynical about people, Elaine. Forgive me. For all I know, Chef Hill is a great humanitarian."

No, Jonathan didn't write the letter, I decided. He was

a kindly, prosperous, much-better-than-average-looking lawyer with a clinging mother.

"Could I interest you in another get-together tonight?" he asked with a sly smile. "Having you all to myself would be a treat for me."

"For me too," I said. "It's a date." If Jonathan had a murderous side, I'd unearth it. If he didn't, I'd let him kiss me some more.

"I'm taking you all for a little spin around the cases here so you'll know what's what," said the chef. "Then we'll hop in the shuttle outside, go back to Whitley's kitchen, and start cooking fish, the whole fish, and nothing but the fish."

I'll spare you his guided tour of Wendell Brothers Fish Market. Suffice it to say that when buying whole fish, pick the ones with bright, clear eyes; for fillets, make sure the flesh isn't faded with age; and for shellfish, only buy from markets with a fast turnover.

By noon we were back in the kitchen, forming a semi-circle around the center island where Chef Hill was demonstrating the method for cutting up a whole halibut so that every conceivable part of the fish could be used, either to make stock or to prepare it for our meal. I'd never seen so many knives. At one point, he wielded a very sharp fish-cutting knife that was as long as a sword and could easily decapitate a person. At another, he used tweezers— "pickers," he called them—to pluck out tiny bones. At another, his tool of choice was a pair of scissors to cut off some of the skin. All of his instruments bore his initials and were in gleamingly pristine condition, including the mallet he would use to make carpaccio later and the mortar and pestle for mashing spices into a paste—all possible weapons of destruction.

"You guys are gonna have a true dock-to-dish meal today, using products from Wendell Brothers market and Whitley Farm as the main ingredients," said Chef Hill. "I'm all about the fresh, people, all about the fresh, so let's get started—bang bang."

First came the fish stock. Chef Hill asked for a helper, and Lake volunteered, of course. While we all looked on, she diced a carrot, a celery stalk, and an onion and sprinkled them into a pot of cold water containing the halibut carcass. Then her job was to bring the water to a simmer for twenty minutes, until the skin flaked away from the bones.

Jonathan was Chef Hill's point man for the bouillabaisse. It was a major job that involved large chunks of the halibut, cod, and snapper and every conceivable type of shellfish, but he was up to the challenge. He even knew how to cut the "beards" off the mussels, and Chef Hill once again told him he should have his own restaurant, which made Beatrice scowl.

Gabriel was designated as the one to pitch in on the achiote-seasoned salmon fillets, which were to be baked inside banana leaves that had been passed over a flame to char and soften them. Alex, Jackie, and Beatrice worked on the fennel-infused rice while Pat, Connie, and Ronnie assembled Chef Hill's crab and avocado appetizer as well as his blueberry tartlets. That left Simon and me to help out with the salmon carpaccio.

"I assume you want me to do the honors with this salmon," he said after Chef Hill stepped away from our station.

"Why, because you think I'm inept?" I said.

"No, because you have an aversion to raw fish, ever since you read that *Daily Beast* article about sushi and parasitic roundworms."

"I'm fine," I said and nudged him away from the counter. I began slicing the salmon into perfectly equal portions, pulling the tip of the knife through the fish with the care of a surgeon.

"Not bad," he said, nodding at my work.

"Thank you." I covered each piece with plastic wrap, as per the recipe, picked up the mallet, and started pounding the crap out of them. I was so unhinged by the letter and its implications that I must have been taking out my anxiety on the poor salmon.

"Hey, easy there, Slim." Simon grabbed the mallet out of my hand and began to strike the pieces less forcefully than I had. "The idea is to flatten them a little, not beat them into submission."

I stepped back and regarded the pieces I'd butchered. They looked like pink Swiss cheese after what I'd done to them, after what a lunatic letter writer had done to me. "I'm sorry. I'm not myself."

Simon focused on making the vinaigrette for the salmon, whisking as he spoke. He was adorable in his apron, the bastard, and as a result I had trouble concentrating on my job, which was preparing a plate of capers and raw red onions for the garnish.

"I see no possible purpose for raw red onions or for capers," I said. "Onions were put on this earth to give us heartburn, and capers are essentially tiny pickles that roll off our knives and forks onto the floor only to get crushed by our feet and then wedged into the soles of our shoes."

Simon looked up at me. "You like capers, so what's really bothering you?"

I hadn't decided whether or not to tell him about the letter, so I said nothing was bothering me and why was he even asking.

He smiled. "Because when there's something sinister and dark going on in that brain of yours, you scrunch up your face and knit your brows together."

"Sounds attractive."

"It is. You are."

"Stop saying things like that."

He went back to whisking, and I went back to contemplating Chef Hill's demise.

"Okay, maybe there is something on my mind," I said, since there didn't seem to be any harm in getting Simon's opinion about the would-be killer—in an abstract way. "Here's a hypothetical question for you. If one of the people here, one of our fellow agritourists, turned out to be a murderer, which one do you think it would be?"

Simon kept on whisking, didn't even flinch. Anyone else would have been thrown by the question, but he knew me, knew how my mind worked, knew that it often went to murder and mayhem for seemingly no reason. "Well, if I had to choose a psycho in this group from what little I know of everybody—just first impressions, you understand—I'd probably choose Jonathan."

"Really? Why?"

"Because he's into you, and you're into him, and I'm jealous."

"Not a good reason. Pick somebody else."

He thought for a minute. "Okay, I pick Beatrice."

"Because?"

"When we were making strawberry crumble together that first day, she was badmouthing Jonathan's cooking hobby without a trace of remorse or shame," he said. "That's one of the common characteristics among psychopaths: lack of remorse or shame."

"Interesting," I said. "Assuming she's capable of murder, what sort of weapon do you think she'd use?"

"I don't see her as a hatchet murderer, and she's unlikely to know anything about explosive devices," he said as he folded the salmon into the vinaigrette. "Strangulation is probably out, too. She has very small hands. If I had to guess, I'd say she'd use either a knife or a gun."

"A gun? You think she owns one?"

"A revolver—a .38 Special."

I tapped him on the shoulder. "When did you get so knowledgeable about guns?"

"You must not be reading my magazine, Slim. I'm hurt and offended." He stuck out his lower lip in a mock pout.

I couldn't help laughing. "Don't tell me. You ran an article about vacation travel involving shooting ranges and gun clubs."

"See that? You did miss it. But I'll forgive you if you tell me why you're asking about all this." He set down the whisk, wiped his hands on his apron, and cocked his head to get a good look at me, his blue eyes roaming my face.

"I saw an episode of *CSI: Cleveland* where somebody in a cooking class was murdered, and I was thinking about it, that's all."

"Nice try, Slim. There is no *CSI: Cleveland.*"

"No? Well, there should be."

He reached for my hand and held it. "Why don't you just tell me about it?"

I wanted to. I really, really wanted to. But Simon Purdys wasn't my go-to guy anymore. "Nothing to tell," I said and left him with the red onions and capers.

18

I made a point of sitting next to Beatrice at the dining table, where we consumed large quantities of our dock-to-dish meal to the point that it would be a very long time before I ate fish again.

"Chef Hill's a terrific cooking instructor," I said to Jonathan's mother as she was tearing off pieces of a crusty French baguette and dipping them in her bouillabaisse broth. She had a great deal of trouble chewing the bread; apparently, she wore dentures and crusty French baguettes were not their friend.

"Silly little man," she said, her words a bit garbled as she continued to wrestle with the bread, dentures be damned. She was perfectly turned out as usual—every silvery hair in place, clothes expensive and without a single wrinkle, make-up expertly applied. If she'd been born in a different time and generation, she would surely have been a Sheryl Sandberg "Lean In" type of woman, the type who asks for raises and sits at the head of the conference table, empowered enough not to have to talk about being empowered. "All those ghastly tattoos. Mr. Hill is a fraud, if you ask me. He makes those obsequious young people do all the work for him. I doubt he can even cook by himself."

You're a fraud—100 percent con artist. That's what the letter said, and now Beatrice had echoed the sentiment.

"What makes you say that?" I asked. "He's taught us all these new techniques. Well, they're new to me anyway."

"I say it because he's running some sort of a conglomerate, but how do we know what Planet Empire really does?" she said. "Arthur, my late husband, used to say that restaurants aren't cash cows."

"So you think Chef Hill has a side business or two?" I asked. "Or maybe a very generous and forgiving backer?"

"I'm just saying that 'Planet Empire' sounds like one of those observatories where people look through telescopes, but what do I know about his business? I've only met the man a half dozen times."

A half dozen times? We'd had three cooking classes with Chef Hill, not six. Had Beatrice run into him prior to the classes at Whitley?

"Do you and Jonathan go to many food and wine events down in Palm Beach?" I asked. I remembered that he went with his mother to her charity events, so maybe she went with him to his.

"Too many," she said. "I have no choice if I want to see my son for more than the five minutes he graces me with on Sunday afternoons."

She sounded like my mother with her "you never call me" whine. The truth was I called my mother nearly every day, just to check in, but it was never enough. "Did Chef Hill appear at any of these events, and did you have a negative experience with him there?" I asked Beatrice.

She stopped chewing and gave me a cold stare. "I thought you said you were in advertising, Elaine."

"PR actually."

"You come off like a prosecutor."

"Sorry." I laughed offhandedly. "My friends call me the Grand Inquisitor. I enjoy getting to know people, that's all."

"Look, let's not beat around the bush." She put down her bread, dabbed at the corners of her mouth with her napkin, and peered at me again. "The person you really want to know is my son—I've seen the two of you making eyes at each other. You're only interested in me so I'll put in a good word for you with him."

Poor Jonathan. Poor, poor Jonathan. She really was a handful, but I played along. "I confess," I said with a girlish giggle. "I do like Jonathan, so it would be wonderful if you'd be in my corner, Beatrice."

She nodded begrudgingly. "At least you earn your own living—enough to be able to afford this ridiculously expensive week—unlike the gold-digger he married last time. I made sure she and his first wife, the doctor, didn't take advantage of his good nature."

"How? I mean what did you do to make sure they didn't?" Shoot them with that .38 Special Simon thinks you own?

"Let's just say I dispensed with them," she said and dove back into the bouillabaisse.

After Beatrice excused herself to repair to her cottage and while Jackie and Pat were focusing on Alex, I went to sit with Connie and Ronnie. The Gumperses must have inhaled the fish courses, because they were well on their way through the blueberry tartlets, which they had buried under an avalanche of whipped cream.

"Has the trip been a fun anniversary celebration for you two?" I asked them.

"Since I *love* to eat, the meals are my favorite part of being an agritourist," said Connie as she shoveled the dessert into her mouth. "I could just skip the cooking and go straight to the food."

"Same here," said Ronnie with a chuckle, "but I'm always hungry after. The portions at this place leave something to be desired."

"And I'm mad at Chef Hill," Connie added. "I'm so nice to him, and he never says anything nice back."

Yup, she's mad at the chef, I thought. But mad enough to kill him? "He's kind of brusque with everyone, not just you, Connie," I said.

"Yeah, but I'm his number one fan," she said, pointing to her *Who wants to get fishy with me* T-shirt. "I've been to his appearances and I watch him on TV and I have all his cookbooks. I even met his wife. She's much nicer than he is. Her name is Kim."

"She's Oriental," said Ronnie, out of breath after inhaling his remaining bites of dessert.

"Asian." Connie elbowed him. "Nobody uses 'Oriental' anymore."

"Not true, Cupcake," he said. "Applebee's uses it. They've had their Oriental chicken salad on the menu for years and I know the description by heart: 'Crisp Oriental greens topped with chunks of crunchy chicken fingers, toasted almonds, and crispy rice noodles tossed in a light

Oriental vinaigrette.' They say 'Oriental' two times right there, not 'Asian.' That's why I like them and Olive Garden and Chico's—none of this farm-to-table bullpucky."

Connie winked at me. "Can't argue with Ronnie when it comes to his favorite restaurants."

"No, you sure can't," I said, because what else can you say?

"I wish somebody would make a movie where the hero orders that Oriental chicken salad," Ronnie mused. "It could be funny, like Jack Nicholson ordering the toast in *Five Easy Pieces*. And while I'm on the subject, how about that restaurant scene in *The Blues Brothers*?" He chuckled again. "Jake and Elwood go to a fancy place like this and order everything on the menu, just so they can get the waiter back in the band. Priceless."

"Ronnie and his movies." Connie sighed. "He can tell you who did what in every one of them."

The letter writer was a movie buff, I recalled. (*"Listen to me carry on about movie villains,"* it said in the very first paragraph.) But what possible motive would Ronnie have for killing Chef Hill?

"Connie, getting back to Chef Hill's wife," I said, "you think she's more gracious toward her husband's fans than he is?"

"Very gracious," she said. "We were at the Chicago food show when I told her how much I loved him. I said, 'If you guys are ever in Kenosha, Wisconsin, you're invited to our house for dinner.' And you know what she said?"

"No," I said, entranced by Connie's mouth. It was rubbery. It moved vertically and horizontally in a way that was startlingly flexible, like a sock puppet.

"'We would love to come. How kind of you, Connie.' That's what she said. And she remembered my name is Connie."

"You were wearing a name tag, Cupcake." Ronnie hiccup-belched.

"I know, but still," said Connie. "Chef Hill never said my name once that day. And now we're here this week. We've had three classes with him so far, and he still acts like he's never met me."

"And you're angry," I confirmed. "Enraged even. Would that be accurate?"

"Yeah, enraged," said Connie. "And I'm telling you, his time is running out."

My pulse quickened. "What do you mean?"

"That I don't stay liking someone forever," she said. "They can hurt my feelings a bunch of times and I'll keep coming back for more—until I reach my limit. And then they're dead to me."

Two conversations had yielded three possible suspects, and I didn't know what to make of the situation. But I had to keep going, keep asking questions. When the Gumperses left the table to get second helpings of dessert, I looked around and noticed that Jackie and Pat weren't in the kitchen, so I decided to squeeze in one more interrogation in their absence.

"Mind if I sit with you?" I said to Lake and Gabriel when I joined them with my plate of blueberry tartlet. They had been arguing. I could feel the chilly air between them.

"No," they said simultaneously in a tone that screamed, "Yes, we mind, but we weren't raised by wolves so we'll be polite and put up with the intrusion."

"Hard to believe there's just one more class to go before the Bounty Fest finale on Saturday," I carried on. "It all went fast, didn't it?"

"Yes," they grunted in unison.

I could see that making conversation with them would be more labor intensive than making cheese. Nevertheless, I tried again. "What do you both think of Chef Hill? He must be a hero of yours, since you're such advocates of the farm-to-table movement."

There was awkward silence until Lake said, as if it were obvious, "Of course he's my hero. He's saving the planet, one mouthful at a time."

Gabriel nodded sourly. "He's Lake's hero all right. Which makes *me* what, exactly? I'll tell you what: I'm just her husband, and husbands don't do anything heroic except pay the bills and make it possible for their wives to volunteer at art museums, have lunch with their girlfriends, and who knows what else when I'm not around."

Whatever they'd been arguing about had him mightily pissed off.

"Don't pay any attention to Gabriel," said Lake when I must have looked uncomfortable. "He's hypoglycemic."

Gabriel laughed scornfully. "Yeah, right. What I am is a hardworking guy who plays by the rules. Vanderkloot here doesn't think I'm out-of-the-box enough."

Undaunted by the fact that Gabriel had just used her maiden name in a derisive tone, Lake turned her lollipop head toward me, calm as can be. "Gabriel and I are having a difference of opinion about a life choice, and he's not handling it well," she explained, as if I were a member of the family instead of a perfect stranger, either because there's a certain intimacy between people who've milked and foraged together, or because they were a strange, strange couple.

"Well, I hope you resolve whatever it is," I said diplomatically, even as I was dying to know if their difference of opinion involved Chef Hill somehow.

"Not likely," said Gabriel, his hawkish eyes boring in on Lake. "She's pretty dug in, and once she is there's no talking her out of it."

"Don't be an asshole," she said. "You were the one who was pretty dug in about not wanting a kid, remember?"

"Yeah, but after I changed my mind, you said you wouldn't take the hormones."

Lake, maintaining her oddly serene demeanor despite his accusations, said, "Why should I pollute my own body with hormones when I won't eat food that's been polluted with hormones? Doesn't make sense at all."

"What doesn't make sense is why you're so reckless about *other things*," he said. "And you know what I'm talking about."

"That's enough." She smacked her hand down on the table, rattling glasses and utensils. So much for the serene demeanor. "I think we should take this back to our cottage now."

"Sure, why not," said Gabriel. "We'll kiss and make up like we always do."

Yeah, they were a weird couple all right. Maybe Gabriel was the one taking hormones. Maybe he was into testosterone and numerous other fitness supplements, and the cocktail was making him violent. Or maybe Lake was the violent one. Maybe they were both nuts enough to kill Chef Hill, although I couldn't figure out why. Oh, this whole thing was exhausting.

19

I called Jonathan when I got back to my cottage to let him know I was free and ready for our date. His phone went straight to voice mail, so I left a message in my most seductive voice suggesting we rendezvous on the terrace again.

While I waited, I decided to do more due diligence than merely google Jonathan. I knew one person in Palm Beach—Olivia Martindale—and it made sense to shoot her an e-mail. Olivia ran Pearson & Strulley's satellite office there, and we'd bumped into each other at various corporate functions over the years. It was her job to know everything about everybody in South Florida, so I asked her for a thumbnail sketch of Jonathan Birnbaum, Esq, explaining that I'd met him on vacation and that a romance between us might be developing. She was British and communicated in clipped, rather abrupt shorthand, but I trusted that she'd tell me if Jonathan had any blemishes on his reputation.

When he returned my call, he asked if we could meet at my cottage instead of on Whitley's terrace—"more private," he said—and I agreed. And then I changed my mind. "You've already seen my digs here. I'd like to see yours." What I wanted to see, of course, were clues that might link Jonathan to the letter.

"My cottage awaits," he said. "Come as soon as you can."

I changed out of the clothes I'd been wearing, since they had a distinctly low-tide smell after all the fish I'd handled, put on a black V-neck top and white jeans, fluffed my hair, applied lipstick and blush, and dabbed a little Shalimar behind my ears.

Not bad, I thought as I gave myself the once-over in the mirror above the sink. *Not Heidi Klum, but good enough not to scare small children.*

"For you," he said when I arrived, presenting me with a bouquet of wildflowers in a pretty earthenware vase. Don't ask me what the flowers were—that was Jackie's domain—but they were bursting with color and very summery.

"Did you pick these yourself?" I asked as I set the flowers on the coffee table. He had showered before I came over, judging by the slight dampness at the ends of his hair.

He chuckled. "I can cook, but my gardening skills are limited. I bought them in the hotel gift shop." He gave me a quick peck on the cheek.

"You're so thoughtful, Jonathan," I said, and meant it. I'm telling you, this guy would not have given me a microwave for my birthday.

"Not thoughtful. I just like you, Elaine. A lot," he said after another quick kiss, this one on the tip of my nose. "I'm hoping this will turn into something."

"But we hardly know each other," I said not for the first time. "And your ex-wives didn't exactly treat you well, from what you told me. Aren't you a little hesitant to jump into another relationship?"

"You're nothing like my ex-wives," he said between nibbles on my neck. "You're steady and dependable."

I laughed. "You make me sound like a Maytag washing machine."

"I just mean that you're someone people can count on. Look at your career. Look at your ability to live on your own. Look at your longstanding friendship with Jackie and Pat, who, by the way, are terrific."

"They are." I snickered to myself, picturing my friends passed out drunk in the car the night before.

Jonathan started to kiss me in earnest, and I was enjoying it until I reminded myself I was supposed to be looking for something incriminating. While his eyes were closed and his hands were roaming my T-shirt, I scanned his cottage. There was a laptop on the desk, but that didn't prove anything, since he was a blogger. There were three of Chef Hill's cookbooks stacked up on the floor, but that didn't prove anything either, since one of them was a souvenir in our tote bags and the other two were on sale at the gift shop.

"Want to dance?" I blurted out, my gaze having landed on the iPod dock on the dresser. I needed to distract him, just long enough to do a little snooping.

"Dance?" he repeated, seeming more interested in undressing me.

"Sure. Come on. Pick out something romantic for us," I said, nodding at the iPod. Normally I was too self-conscious to dance—tall people like me aren't always the most graceful—but I had a job to do.

"Whatever makes you happy," said Jonathan, tearing himself away from me to find us some music.

While he was otherwise engaged, I casually inched over to the stack of cookbooks and opened one, just because I thought it was a little odd that he owned so many by a chef he was clearly ambivalent about. And the book covers were tattered and worn, not pristine the way they should have been if he'd just bought them. Had he already owned them and schlepped them from Palm Beach in his luggage, and if so why?

I flipped through the pages and was surprised how marked up they were; Jonathan had highlighted some chapters, drawn arrows pointing to other sections, and written comments next to many of them. Was it simply that there were certain recipes he'd tried at home and wanted to ask Chef Hill about? He interrupted my snooping before I could get a close look at the words he'd written.

"How about this?" he asked, referring to the music. "An oldie."

I quickly closed the book and composed my face into what I hoped was a sex kitten look.

"Elvis," he said when the song started to play. He beckoned me to him, held me tightly around my waist, brought his face close to mine, and starting humming as we moved side to side. "'Can't Help Falling in Love with You.' Apropos song title, maybe?"

"Um hmm," I said noncommittally. My mother used to listen to Elvis's records while she was ironing, and she would imitate his hip swivel. She had a sense of humor when she wasn't railing against my father.

As Jonathan resumed dotting my neck with kisses and

the occasional flick of his tongue, my mind continued to wander. Could he really be a murderer? He seemed like such a dear man, and he liked me. But just to be safe, I peppered him with questions about Chef Hill as we danced. Was he angry with the chef for denigrating food bloggers? Did he think the chef was a fraud, the way the letter writer did? Did he come to Cultivate Our Bounty week to take farm-to-table cooking classes and fulfill his summer travel obligation to his mother or did he have another purpose in coming? He asked why I was asking, but gave me satisfactory answers to the first two questions. And then he smiled at the last one.

"Yes, I did have another purpose in coming to Whitley." He stopped dancing and gazed into my eyes. Our bodies were pressed together, and I felt his erection. Oh God.

"Another purpose?" I said, trying to ignore the fact that he was aroused in the middle of my interrogation.

"Don't laugh, but I think I came here to meet Elaine Zimmerman," he said, his own eyes hooded with desire. "I think it was our destiny to meet."

Let me say a few words about destiny: I don't believe in it. I also don't believe in one door closing and another door opening. I don't believe in everything happening for a reason, either. I believe that we go along and work hard and do the best we can, and sometimes it goes well and sometimes it doesn't and that's just how it is. As far as Jonathan Birnbaum was concerned, I believed that we met because we both happened to write a big fat check to Whitley Farm for the same week. But of course I didn't say so. I said, "All I know is this trip has taken some turns I wasn't expecting, and you're one of them, Jonathan."

We kissed and pawed each other as we danced, but my

heart wasn't really in it. There were too many uncertainties buzzing around in my head.

I told Jonathan I needed a bathroom break. "The heat and humidity," I said by way of explanation instead of the truth, which was that I wanted to do more snooping. "I drank a lot of water today."

"I'll be waiting," he said, his face glowing with anticipation.

I took a look around the fancy bathroom with no idea what I was expecting to find. I opened the vanity drawers and didn't come upon anything remarkable. I checked the inside of the shower and there was nothing of interest there, unless Jonathan was planning to kill Chef Hill with his Gillette Mach 3 Turbo razor. I spotted his brown leather Dopp kit and peeked inside. Along with his deodorant, nail clippers, and cologne were bottles of pills—the usual meds for a man of his age: Norvasc, Lipitor, Nexium and—wait—*four bottles of Vicodin? Each Vicodin prescription filled at a different pharmacy in Palm Beach? Each written for Beatrice Birnbaum?*

I was dumbfounded, naturally. What was Jonathan doing with four bottles of an opiate that weren't even his? Was he an addict, pretending to be his mother's caregiver, filling her prescriptions for her arthritis pain medication and keeping them for himself? Or had he been stockpiling the pills expressly for this trip? Maybe his plan was to come to Whitley, wait until Bounty Fest, force the whole stash down Chef Hill's throat at gunpoint and cause him to overdose.

"Don't be too long, Elaine," Jonathan called out. "I miss you."

Right. Right. I was supposed to be peeing. I ran the water in the sink, flushed the toilet, rinsed my hands and wiped them on a towel. And then I took a deep breath and sashayed back out there.

Jonathan encircled me in his arms. He had turned off the music and was now walking me toward the bed, serious intent in his eyes—and in his pants. "If it's too soon, tell me," he murmured.

"Too soon," I said quickly. Having sex with a possible husband would have been permissible, if a little promiscuous after only one date, but having sex with a possible murderer? Not a chance. "I mean, I really like being with you, Jonathan, but I think we should take it slower."

"I understand." He settled for sitting me down at the end of the bed instead of throwing me down and mounting me. "It's just that we're heading toward the end of our week here, and I feel the clock ticking."

"You and me both," I said, thinking of poor Chef Hill, for whom Saturday was D Day unless my friends and I intervened. I needed to talk to them ASAP and tell them what I found out. I looked at my watch. "Damn." I bolted up, nearly head-butting Jonathan. "I'm so sorry. I just remembered I'm supposed to call a client in five minutes— major PR disaster, you have no idea—and I have to get back to my cottage so I'll have my notes in front of me."

"But it's late," Jonathan pointed out. "And you're on vacation."

"I'm never really on vacation, total workaholic, and the client is three hours earlier in California, Hollywood type," I said, grasping for even a semi-plausible explanation for my behavioral about-face. "She's—well, let's just say she's the star of a very popular TV series on Netflix."

Jonathan perked up. "It's not by any chance Robin Wright? She's brilliant on *House of Cards.*"

"Okay, yes, it's Robin Wright," I lied. "But please don't tell anyone, because she'd fire me if she thought I was betraying a confidence." My most high-profile celebrity client at the moment was a seventeen-year-old video gamer with over two million followers on Twitter.

"Of course," he said. "Attorney-client privilege, right?"

"Exactly. Gotta go. But we'll pick this up again tomorrow?"

"You bet," he said as I hurried toward the door. Between the weirdness of all the cookbooks and the giant supply of Vicodin, I couldn't get out of there fast enough.

"Thank you for the flowers and the dancing," I said as we stood in his doorway. "You were sweet to have me over."

"Nothing 'sweet' about it," said Jonathan. "I wanted to be with my new lady."

His new lady, I thought as I left. Was that what I was? Maybe, if he didn't turn out to be a cold-blooded killer.

20

"What do you make of it all?" I asked Jackie and Pat when we convened at my cottage.

"Pill popper," said Jackie, referring to the Vicodin.

"I never would have guessed," Pat said after a tsk-tsk. "He seemed so nice."

"He's still nice," said Jackie. "But he should be at a rehab place instead of a farm resort. None of this links him to the letter though."

"And the cookbooks he brought with him from home could just mean he really does want to be a chef," said Pat. "He probably reads recipes the way Bill reads medical case histories."

"I hope he's not a pill popper." I sighed, flashing back to my intimate moments with Jonathan. "I can't get involved with a drug addict. I have my limits."

"We struck out with Alex," said Jackie. "All she did was talk about her screenplay."

"And dental hygiene," said Pat. "She told us the difference between calculus and plaque."

Jackie yawned. "We'll have better luck tomorrow when we're all cooking together. Oh, and I'm planning to get Kevin's take on the people in our group."

"Who the hell is Kevin?" I asked.

"The hot gardener in charge of the foraging lesson," she said. "He helped out when Beatrice did her 'I've fallen and I can't get up' routine."

I shrugged. "Sure, why not."

"I still think you should ask Simon to help," Pat said to me.

"And I think we should all go to bed," I said, not having the energy to revisit that conversation.

We said goodnight and pledged to get to the bottom of the letter when we were fresher in body and mind.

"Don't forget to lock your doors," I told my friends as they were leaving. "Rebecca's idyllic place isn't so idyllic after all."

Alone at last, I changed into my nightgown, a very short pink cotton number that fell about mid-thigh. I only resorted to wearing it in hot, humid weather, because it exposed so much of my legs and made me look like a stork, but who cared. No one would see me.

At least that's what I thought. No sooner did I wash my face, apply moisturizer, and put my night guard in, the one that kept my teeth from grinding themselves into dust while I slept, than I heard a knock at the door.

I considered not answering it. I considered calling the front desk. I considered screaming, "Help!" It was much too late for visitors, so I was sure it was the killer who'd found out I'd been snooping and come to carve me up with a bread knife.

I peeked out the side window and saw it was only Simon. Since he was the lesser of two evils, I let him in.

"Whaareyoudoinghere?" I said.

He pointed to my mouth. "Could you take that thing out so we can talk?"

"Oh. Right." I pried out the night guard and put it in its little plastic case in the bathroom. By the time I was back, Simon was hanging his black rain slicker on the hook in the entryway. I'd been so focused on the murder business that I'd completely ignored the fact that it had started to thunder—the first storm of our week at Whitley. There was lightning, too, and the rain was intensifying—summer storms often flared up in the heat only to peter out an hour or two later. "And the reason for this drop-in? Are you writing a piece about an agritourist who would rather go to sleep than rehash the same old argument with—"

He didn't let me finish. Instead he pulled me into his arms and kissed me, and I nearly passed out from the sheer exquisiteness of his mouth on mine. This was nothing like what Jonathan and I had been doing. This was the real thing, the thing I'd missed more than I'd wanted to admit, and I couldn't allow myself to get sucked back into it.

I started to push Simon away the minute our lips made contact again, but like many a heroine of a romantic melodrama, I succumbed and fell deeply into the kiss, into his arms. We stayed in the entryway like that—kissing and taking a breath and then kissing some more—for at least ten minutes before he finally took my hand and led me to the bed. It occurred to me that I should have shaved my legs. It occurred to me that I should have worn something sexier than the stork nightie. It occurred to me that I should have skipped the moisturizer, which was rich and creamy but left a residue wherever it landed. In this case on Simon's shirt.

"What's the point of this?" I said as he lowered me down onto the bed.

"No analyzing. Let's just be together, Slim, and the future will take care of itself, okay?"

The future involved the murder of a famous chef and anyone else who happened to be in the vicinity, so the present was infinitely more appealing. "Okay," I said, feeling my body open up to the man I couldn't have stopped loving no matter how hard I tried.

"I love you," he murmured as he lifted the nightgown over my head. "You make me crazy, but I love you."

"Same here," I said as I unzipped his jeans. I used to think of myself as a non-sexual person before I met Simon. The sort of throbbing, soaking wet, multiple orgasms, transcendent sensory experience that other women raved about had escaped me. And then Simon and I made love for the first time on the *Princess Charming* and I thought: This *is what they're all talking about. This is why they can't get enough of it. This is what they mean by "great sex."* Not only was Simon an expert at lovemaking, but he made me feel desired and cherished when we made love. And another thing: he made me feel safe—not a bad way to feel, under the circumstances.

Day Five:
Friday, July 19

21

"Did you know that mosquitoes are attracted to people who give off carbon dioxide during exertion?" said Simon as he was pulling on his jeans, tucking in his shirt, and watching me at the same time. "So try to keep the heavy breathing to a minimum."

The rain had given way to an oppressively hot and sticky morning with the threat of more thunder showers forecasted for later in the day. I dressed accordingly in a light, loose-fitting tunic and capri pants, and slathered myself in both sunscreen and insect repellent.

"Thanks for the tip," I said, wondering if I'd be exerting myself and breathing heavily as I was fending off a crazed letter writer. Yes, Simon and I had shared a blissful night together, and being with him had helped me block out visions of death and destruction, for which I was grateful, but nothing had changed between us. He hadn't proposed either before or after our athletic sex or indicated that he would when we got back to New York. And so I had vowed yet again to move on without him. Still, I couldn't deny the wisdom of telling him about the letter and letting him offer another point of view.

When he was ready to leave the cottage, he stroked my cheek tenderly. "I guess you'll go back to ignoring me today?"

"Actually, no," I said. "Could you sit a minute? I could use your input."

His brows furrowed and he settled into one of the chairs. "You're in trouble. All those who-could-be-a-murderer questions while we were making salmon carpaccio weren't just small talk. Am I right?"

I pulled the letter out of the dresser drawer and handed it to him.

He read it quietly and then said with a headshake, "Jesus, people are really nuts."

I filled him in on the failed attempts to get Chef Hill, Rebecca, and the police to take the letter seriously. I also told him what Jackie, Pat and I knew about the members of our Cultivate Our Bounty group. I even admitted I'd been digging around in Jonathan's cottage during my date with him last night.

He looked wounded. "You were with both of us?"

"Not the way you mean." I was many things, but a slut was not one of them. "The headline is that Jonathan had four vials of Vicodin with his mother's name on the prescriptions. They were right there in his bathroom. If he's a drug addict, he could be so addled that he wrote the letter to Chef Hill and didn't know what he was doing."

I sat in the other chair and waited for Simon to respond to my theory.

"Far be it from me to praise the guy, since he wants to get in your pants," he said, "but he's no druggie."

"And you know this because...."

"Remember when I told you Beatrice and I had a little heart-to-heart the other day? Well, in between criticizing Jonathan for wanting to be a chef, she criticized him for confiscating her pills. She went on quite the tirade about how controlling he was. She said he was a lawyer, not a doctor, and who was he to decide what she needed for her back pain and how much was too much. Bottom line? Your boyfriend's a good son for trying to protect his mother from herself."

"That's a relief."

"Doesn't mean he didn't write this letter though."

Simon read it again. Then he and I went down the list of the other group members and speculated about which of them might be "enraged" enough to murder Chef Hill at Saturday's Bounty Fest.

"I'll call Larry," he said, referring to his boss, a corpulent, much-divorced man whose family owned several magazines, including *Away from It All*. Larry was always threatening to fire people but was really just horny. "He eats at Jason Hill's restaurant at least three times a week. Maybe he knows something about the guy."

"Worth a shot."

"And I'll find out if any of my reporters have done a travel story on Kenosha, Wisconsin," he added. "They might have sources who know Ronnie and Connie."

"'Sources.' I like when you talk like a journalist."

"And I like when you include me in your madcap adventures."

"Some adventure. I don't mind telling you this whole

thing scares me," I said, hoping he would put his arms around me, which he did.

"I won't let anybody hurt you, Slim. You know that."

You hurt me, I thought, but didn't say. My heartache seemed like small potatoes in the grand scheme of things.

22

"Here we are for our last class of the week," said Chef Hill from behind the center island as we all sat in our seats. He was twitchy, hyperkinetic, moving around so fast that it was unnerving to try to follow him. I wondered how much of his supposed fortune paid for his cocaine habit and whether he had to cut corners in his business, make compromises, make enemies in order to keep the white stuff in ample supply. "We're gonna do chocolate desserts today, gang, and not just any chocolate desserts, or they wouldn't be farm-to-table. I didn't get a reputation in the food world by turning out Hershey's bars, you know? Not that I'm here to knock mass-produced name brands. They serve their purpose. But do they serve the planet and the farmers? Offer us a sustainable, healthy alternative? Taste as pure and clean as possible? Not a chance. My chocolate desserts may be rich and not for the calorie conscious, but they're desserts you can feel good about. They're the ecstasy without the guilt—bang bang."

The plan for the first part of the day's cooking class was for the Three Blonde Mice to grill our designated suspects, even if it meant going back over territory we'd already covered with them. Jackie would focus on Lake, Gabriel, and Alex, Pat would interrogate Connie, Ronnie, and Beatrice, and I would have Jonathan to myself. Simon, meanwhile, would duck in and out of class in order to work his contacts. The ducking in and out wouldn't be easy for him, because he loved chocolate with the blinding passion I'd hoped he'd have for me. If chocolate were a woman, he wouldn't have been "almost ready" to marry it.

"The foundation for the chocolates we're making today is Whitley's milk," the chef continued, with more seriousness of purpose than he'd shown in previous classes. Or maybe he was just happy that his week of being stuck with us was coming to an end, and he wanted to go out with a bang bang. "Whitley's milk, along with their butter and cream, is something special, as you found out, so our chocolate desserts today, coming from that sweet, fresh milk, will be amazing. In addition to the candy-type items we'll be showing you, I'll be sharing the recipe for my exclusive signature dessert, the same dessert I've been serving at The Grow since the first restaurant opened. It's my dark chocolate marquise with beet cremeux, beet-and-raspberry sauce, and salted pistachio croquant."

We all looked at each other as if he'd been speaking Swahili.

"Sorry. Didn't mean to confuse you people." He laughed. He really was in better humor. "A chocolate marquise is basically a rich chocolate mousse, but it's dense enough to be sliced and served like a cake. Cremeux is a fancy French word for a creamy pudding." He placed his hand on his heart and sighed. "Oh man, do I love pudding. I'm a total pudding freak."

My friends and I went rigid at the mention of the nickname the killer had given Chef Hill—the killer who was sitting right in our midst, inches away, for God's sake. Why oh why hadn't we decided to do a week at a spa like normal women?

"A croquant is another fancy French word," he chatted away. "It means 'crisp' and it's made with nuts and caramelized sugar and crumbled over a dessert or eaten like brittle. Now if you're asking yourself, 'Why is he putting beets in his chocolate dessert?' the answer is simple. Beets are sweet and earthy and marry beautifully with chocolate, but my whole purpose for promoting earthy desserts is to show respect and appreciation for farm ingredients and the men and women who grow them."

There was applause, and then Chef Hill got cooking. Since it was our last class, he said it would be a demonstration as opposed to an actual cooking class, and that we should move from station to station and observe. His assistants would be making the candies: dark chocolate peanut butter bonbons, dark chocolate bark with ginger, macadamia nuts and coconut, and dark chocolate almond date balls. He would be concocting his signature dish, the dark chocolate marquise, himself.

I glommed onto Jonathan, who had staked out a prime spot for the marquise-watching.

"Hello you," he said as Chef Hill began with the crust for the dessert, which entailed melting chocolate and cocoa butter and chilling it until firm. "I had fun dancing with you last night."

"Me too," I said.

"Did you straighten everything out with Robin Wright?"

"Robin Wright?" I almost forgot my own bullshit. "Oh, Robin. Sure. Thanks for asking."

"While you were talking to a glamorous movie star, I stayed up to write my blog," said Jonathan. "I had some new recipes I wanted to post."

"Were they inspired by Chef Hill's recipes?" *Like maybe you've been copying them directly from his cookbooks?*

I waited for him to answer until I realized he was busy watching Chef Hill make the marquise part of the dessert. So I watched, too, as the chef melted more chocolate and butter, whipped egg whites, stirred egg yolks into the chocolate mixture, folded in the egg whites, and poured it all into the chilled crust.

"No, they're recipes I've been playing with on my own," he replied when there was a break in the action. "I'd love to make them for you when you come to Palm Beach." His expression saddened. "We don't have much time left here, and I'm not crazy about having to say goodbye to you, Elaine. Tomorrow will be a zoo, and then we all leave on Sunday."

If we're still alive. "Are you looking forward to Bounty Fest?"

"Not really. I've had enough of our chef at this point."

"But he keeps complimenting your work and saying you should go pro. I've heard him. And you're so into his classes."

He didn't answer right away. He was concentrating on the way Chef Hill was putting together the beet cremeux, which involved extracting beet juice with a juicer and combining it with mascarpone cheese, heavy cream, and powered sugar.

"Jason Hill is talented and entrepreneurial, and I can't help but envy him a little," he said. "I didn't mean to suggest I wasn't grateful for whatever praise he doles out."

So Jonathan envied Chef Hill. So what? It wasn't as if he were some ne'er-do-well without any talents of his own. He was a partner in a law firm. Plus, he was way better looking than Jason Hill and probably had his pick of Palm Beach socialites now that he was single again.

He placed his hand on my back as we watched Chef Hill make the beet-and-raspberry sauce for the dessert, followed by the salted pistachio croquant. I asked him more questions. Was he a letter writer? (He preferred texting.) Was he up on movie villains? (He was more of a reader than a moviegoer.) Did he bring a printer with him for his laptop? (He didn't.) I kept trying to drag pertinent information out of him, and he kept trying to watch Chef Hill cook.

"It all looks good enough to eat," I said as I trailed behind him. He was eager to move around the kitchen now, surveying the scene as Chef Hill's assistants performed their respective tasks. "Beets with chocolate in that marquise thing. Who'd have put those two together, right?"

"Chocolate pairs well with lots of foods," said Jonathan. "And beets are so sweet that they add to the richness of the cake."

"So you've cooked with beets a lot?" I asked him.

"Many times," said Jonathan. "With and without chocolate."

"You have all of Chef Hill's cookbooks too," I said.

"I do," said Jonathan. "I'm such a geek I brought my old copies with me so I could reread his best recipes."

So much for the theory that the cookbooks had anything to do with Jonathan wanting to murder the chef.

During the break between the cooking of chocolates and the eating of the meal being prepared by Chef Hill and his staff, my friends and I huddled outside the kitchen and compared notes.

"You were right about Lake and Gabriel, Elaine," said Jackie after I filled them in on my non-informative conversation with Jonathan. "Definitely a weird vibe there. He's mad at her for being 'out of control' and she's mad at him for being 'conventional.' She might even have used the word 'bourgeois.' I got the feeling she wanted him to do something and he was resisting. She made a crack about how he wasn't very open-minded."

"Maybe she wants to become a vegan and he doesn't think it's a good idea," said Pat. "Bill believes that—"

"I thought you were gonna stop dragging him into every conversation," Jackie groused.

"I was talking about Bill Clinton," said Pat. "He's a vegan."

"Somehow I doubt the Vanderkloot-Arnolds were squabbling over tofu," I said. "I wish we knew if it had anything to do with Chef Hill."

"I tried," said Jackie. "I also asked if they checked into the hotel early, before the rest of us got here on Monday. I wanted to find out if either of them had access to those tote bags, like if one of them was looking for Chef Hill's bag, heard somebody coming, and stuffed the letter in yours in the rush to get out of there without being caught."

"And what did they say?" I asked.

"Yes, they got here early," she said. "They also admitted to being under a lot of stress lately, but what does it all prove?"

I sighed. "Not much, I guess, except that we can't rule either of them out as suspects. Did you get anything interesting on the Gumperses, Pat?"

"Just things we already knew," she replied. "Connie's mad at the chef for not acknowledging what a fan she is. Ronnie's definitely not a fan. He hates all this 'sissy food,' he called it."

"And Beatrice?" I asked, since she was Pat's responsibility, too.

"She needs one of those anger management courses," she said. "She's angry that Jonathan is thinking of quitting his law practice. She's angry that Chef Hill complimented his cooking skills, and she's really angry that her husband died and left her alone. She talked about what a perfect marriage they had. 'We never had a single cross word,' she said. 'Not one fight—ever.'"

"Now that's the first real piece of incriminating evidence against her," I said. "No one has a perfect marriage. She has to be lying right there."

"*Elaine*," said Jackie and Pat simultaneously.

"I'm sorry, but none of it proves she wrote the letter," I pointed out. "Jackie, did you get anywhere with Alex?"

"She's been trying to score a one-on-one with Chef Hill for her screenplay research," she said. "She asked him twice if he'd give her an interview tomorrow at Bounty Fest."

"Aha!" I said. "The crazed letter writer plans to kill him

at Bounty Fest! I was sort of figuring Alex was innocent, but we might have a match!"

"She's a dental hygienist with a nice fiancé," said Jackie. "She's no murderer."

"Number one, how do you know her fiancé is nice?" I said. "Number two, how do you know she's not a murderer? She wears bandanas."

"*Elaine.*" They both groaned.

"Hey, she's the only one who's admitted to wanting Chef Hill all to herself," I said.

"For like twenty minutes," said Jackie.

"It doesn't take long to pull the trigger or hack someone with a meat cleaver," I said.

"I can't see it," said Jackie, shaking her head. "I also spoke to Kevin, the forager. He reminded me about the amaranth."

"What about it?" I said.

"That it can cause toxicity if eaten in large amounts. Remember how Lake and Gabriel were such experts in how to cook and eat it? We need to get into their cottage and see if they have bags of it."

"Right," said Pat. "Maybe their plan all along has been to keep putting it in Chef Hill's food until it kills him."

"Then why would the letter mention Bounty Fest?" Jackie pointed out.

"By the way, have you slept with Kevin yet?" I teased her.

She shook her head. "My sex drive seems to have died. Murder does that to me."

She was getting antsy, fidgety, walking around in tight little circles, and it was contagious. Pat and I started following her, and we looked like a trio of hamsters in a cage. "Somebody in our group has a grudge against Chef Hill and I can't believe we haven't noticed it," she said.

"We've noticed Connie's grudge," said Pat. "She told us she's mad at him. And Beatrice. She doesn't like him either."

I stopped pacing and put my hands on my friends' shoulders to stop them from pacing too. We were expending valuable energy. "And Jonathan doesn't like him because he puts down food bloggers," I said. "So what?" I threw up my hands in frustration.

Just then, Simon raced over us. He was out of breath, just like he'd been after our sexual acrobatics the night before. "I spoke to Larry," he said referring to his boss. "He told me Jason Hill is having an affair with his sous-chef."

"Male or female?" I asked.

"What difference does it make?" said Jackie.

"Just from a PR standpoint," I explained. "Nobody's surprised when chefs sleep around, so if the sous-chef is female, it's kind of a nonstory. But if the sous-chef is a guy and Chef Hill turns out to be gay after claiming to be such a family man, it's a bigger deal. Remember the letter? It said the chef had too many secrets of his own to contact the cops. Maybe his affair with the sous-chef is one of the secrets."

"This is all fascinating, Slim, but the sous-chef is female," said Simon. "Larry told me Chef Hill is having an affair with his investments advisor too—also female."

"How does he have the time to fucking cook?" asked Jackie. "Maybe it's his wife who wants to kill him. I would."

"She's probably one of those celebrity wives who enjoy the perks of being married to a famous person so they look the other way," I said. "But maybe Connie found out about his indiscretions and got angry on the wife's behalf."

"Speaking of the Gumperses, one of my reporters does have a source in Kenosha," said Simon. "Turns out Ronnie's the one with a temper. He got into a physical altercation with a neighbor. It made the front page of the *Kenosha News*."

"Must have been a slow news day," I said. "What was the fight about?"

"Ronnie left an old washing machine on his front lawn for weeks, hoping somebody would buy it," said Simon. "The neighbor told him it was an eyesore and so was the old Barcalounger he'd left on the lawn the month before. Fisticuffs ensued."

"Was Ronnie arrested?" Pat asked? "He could be a rapper."

"You mean he could have a rap sheet." I turned to Simon. "Does he?"

"No," said Simon. "The neighbor declined to press charges."

"Okay, enough with all this conjecture," I said, throwing up my hands again. "Let's do some real digging."

"How?" said Pat. "I'm out of questions to ask them."

"I mean digging, as in digging around in their cottages while they're not there."

"You're not talking about breaking in?" Pat's eyes bugged out.

"That's exactly what I'm talking about. The housekeepers are constantly coming around with fresh towels and soaps and lotions. The keys sit right on top of their carts. I've seen them. I say we just go in and ransack."

"Yeah, let's ransack," said Jackie. "Maybe we'll find the murder weapon."

"I'm in," said Pat.

"Good idea. Bad execution," said Simon. "If all three of you are out of the kitchen at the same time, people will get suspicious." He nodded at Jackie and Pat. "I'll slip out with Elaine while you two cover for us. Just keep the others busy enough not to notice we're gone."

"Jonathan will notice," I said. "He likes me, remember?"

"If he asks, Jackie and Pat can say you had a PR emergency," Simon suggested.

"Right," I said. "Tell him I had another crisis with Robin Wright."

23

Since this was the last sit-down meal with the members of our agritourism group, and since Whitley really wanted to showcase their bounty, the non-dessert portion of our meal prepared by Chef Hill and his assistants was a farm-to-table, dock-to-table, barn-to-table extravaganza.

For our first course we were served a carrot—unpeeled, unadorned, and unaccompanied by anything else—and it was the sweetest single carrot I'd ever tasted.

"What a joke," said Ronnie, whose dissatisfaction with Chef Hill's food philosophy was becoming more and more apparent. In a demonstration of protest, he snapped the carrot in two and shoved his plate aside, only to reconsider and gobble up both carrot halves in one mouthful.

Next came a salad, which consisted of exactly two cherry tomatoes, two radishes, and two types of lettuce, all dressed in nasturtium vinaigrette. The dish was nearly as spare as the carrot but it, too, was bursting with flavor. All fads and preciousness aside, both courses were delicious.

A cucumber gazpacho followed, as did hay-roasted asparagus topped with the yoke of an egg, halibut braised in duck fat and served on a bed of kale, three different cuts of Berkshire pork each dotted with a single artichoke, and fennel sausage garnished with pickled fern fronds and garbanzo beans—all beautifully presented and tasty, but I couldn't let myself get distracted.

The plan was for me to sneak out during dessert, since we knew that it consisted of many chocolate courses, including Chef Hill's signature dark chocolate marquise, and that it would take awhile. And there would be endless conversations of the type that occur at the end of a shared vacation experience—exchanges of e-mail addresses and pledges to get together that would never happen. Simon would follow me out, and Jackie and Pat would make absolutely sure that everybody else stayed put.

"I'm not happy about missing all the chocolate," Simon whispered in my ear.

"I'll buy you a Milky Way if we get out of this place alive," I whispered back.

I snuck out during the first chocolate course and followed the path to the cottages. I knew where the other agritourists were staying because I'd been to Jonathan's cottage, Pat had asked Connie and Ronnie for their cottage number, and Jackie had asked Lake, Gabriel, and Alex for theirs. Fortunately, they were all clustered in the same area of the resort. I had input the information on my phone, which I powered up as soon as I stepped outside.

I approached the Gumpers's cottage first, since it was the closest to the kitchen, and ran smack into a housekeeper wheeling a cart.

"Good afternoon," she said.

"Same to you," I said, noting not for the first time that Whitley Farm housekeepers were not only friendly but also well-dressed. No chintzy uniforms for them. They wore smart-looking gray dresses with short white bib aprons that had lace trim around their two front pockets.

"I am Sonia," she said.

I didn't want to be rude even though I didn't have time to chat, so I said, "I am Elaine," in an unconscious mimicking of her charmingly Slavic accent.

"I like purple top," she said.

"This?" I pointed to my oversized blouse, which was long enough to resemble a caftan. It was pale lavender, had three buttons in the front, and was made of some light, gauzy fabric that didn't make me sweat like a Berkshire pig in the summer. I wore it over jeans and camisoles, in this case white ones.

"Yes," she said. "I like."

"Thank you."

"Do you enjoy stay?" she asked.

"Very much," I said, tantalizingly close to the Gumpers's front door and impatient to get to it, knowing Simon was probably on his way. I glanced at Sonia's cart and didn't see a single set of keys. Not on top of the boxes of tissues. Not dangling from a dust mop. Not nestled in a pile of fresh towels. A change of tactic was in order. "Sonia, I wonder if you could help me out. I seem to have forgotten my key." I nodded at the Gumpers's cottage. "Could you let me in? I'll only need a few minutes."

She smiled. She was missing an incisor, poor thing. Didn't a socially enlightened institution like Whitley provide its employees with dental coverage? "This not your cottage, Elaine," she said oddly but, of course, accurately.

"Sure it is," I said. She'd never seen me before and vice versa. On the other hand, she may very well have seen the Gumperses go in and out.

Sonia shook her head, her hair platinum blonde with black roots. "It belong to fatty peoples. Very nice. Leave good tips."

The Gumperses were tipping already? I never tipped housekeepers at hotels until I checked out. I'd always leave some cash on the dresser next to the TV remote and then wonder if it was enough. "Okay, yes. You must mean Connie and Ronnie. They're friends of mine. They asked me to come and get something they left behind this morning. We've been cooking chocolate desserts today. I wish I'd brought you a chocolate peanut butter ball."

Sonia stood there with a skeptical look. "Can't let guest into other guest's cottage. Don't want to lose job," she said. "Have two kids and husband that love vodka."

I took the liberty of reaching out to touch Sonia's arm in a gesture I hoped would convey my sisterly empathy. "I feel your pain. I have a boyfriend who's afraid to get married," I said.

"Give me purple top," she said as if she were making perfect sense.

"Purple top," I repeated because I still wasn't grasping the situation.

"Don't have money to buy nice clothes." She pointed to my blouse. "So I take top and you take key to cottage."

She was giving me the key? "I thought you were worried about losing your job, Sonia."

"I am excellent housekeeper, Elaine. Won't lose job." She clucked with the confidence of someone who made shakedown deals like this every day.

"I don't know. The top is my favorite piece of clothing. It has sentimental value," I said, deciding to up the stakes since she was willing to bargain. Nothing ventured and all that. "My mother got it for me for Christmas, the day before she fell and shattered her hip, had a stroke, and lost the ability to speak. She can only blink when I visit. She's in a nursing home now and, well, let's just say it breaks my heart every time I see her." My mother was in perfect health and I hoped I hadn't just jinxed her. "So I'll give you the top if you give me the keys to all the cottages, not just this one."

She arched her right eyebrow, which, by the way, was as black as her roots. "All cottages? What for? You are thief, Elaine?"

"Hardly," I scoffed. "I'm a guest here." I pulled my own key out of my jeans pocket and showed it to her. "It's just that it's almost the end of the Cultivate Our Bounty week at Whitley and I've gotten very close to the other guests I've been cooking with. I wanted to leave each of them a surprise in their cottages—a handwritten note telling them how much I enjoyed the time with them."

"Why not leave notes at front desk?"

"Too impersonal," I said.

"No. Can't give you all keys," she said.

"No keys, no purple top," I said, amazing myself with my brazenness. Still, I had nothing to lose except a two-year-old article of clothing purchased at Bloomies during their 20 percent off friends and family sale.

"Okay, okay. You give me top, I give you keys," she said.

"I finished cleaning cottages for today anyway. You return keys to housekeeping office when you finish, and I go home to kids and drunk husband."

"Oh, thank you, Sonia. Thank you very much," I said, thrilled that she was agreeing to hand me access to the personal belongings of all the suspects. "Just one thing: If I give you my top, what will I wear?"

She untied her white bib apron and shoved it into my arms. "I'm done today. Don't need. Put it over camisole and say you're housekeeper if anybody asks."

"Good thinking." I pulled the blouse over my head and exchanged garments with Sonia. All things considered, it seemed like a win-win.

"Too bad they don't pay me to think," she said.

"Where's the housekeeping office for when I return the keys?" I asked when I'd finished outfitting myself in her bib. I looked like I'd wandered in from Red Lobster.

"Over there." She nodded toward a weathered barn that presumably was not populated by cows or chickens. "Return keys and keep apron for funny souvenir from vacation. Hotel has plenty more." She laughed and took off.

"What's with the outfit?" said Simon as he popped up next to me while I was trying to open the Gumpers's door. The lock needed some WD-40. "Not that I mind it," he went on, appraising my apron. "Just the opposite. It's like one of those French maid costumes only without the little skirt."

"I'd explain, but it'll take too long," I said, opening the door at last. "Let's get started."

The Gumperses weren't the neat freaks I was. Their cottage was strewn with discarded clothes, wet towels, and empty packages of Doritos, Cheetos, strawberry Pop Tarts, and beef jerky.

Wishing I'd brought surgical gloves, I began to pick through their detritus in search of any hint that one of them had written the letter to Chef Hill, while Simon poked around in the dresser and closet for concealed weapons. He didn't find any. We looked for DVDs of *Terminator 2* and *Ghostbusters*, the movies mentioned in the poison pen letter, and didn't find those either.

"They've got matching laptops," I said, pointing to the desk, "But there's no printer, so how did the letter find its way into my tote bag?"

"Maybe they used the printer in Whitley's business center," said Simon. "Or more likely, they wrote the letter before coming here."

"Oh wow. Look at this, Simon." I waved him over to Connie's computer. There was a folder marked "Chef Hill" in which there were scanned copies of his biography, his tour itinerary, his TV appearances, and his headshot.

He leaned in closer to examine the photo. "She put an *x* across his face."

"My God. Who does that?" I said, my heart pounding. "Somebody who wants the person in the photograph dead, that's who."

"It does make her seem a little deranged." He moved on to Ronnie's laptop. After a few clicks of the mouse, he opened a Word document entitled 'Hit List.' "Looks like he put together the names of the chefs who were voted the top farm-to-table chefs in America."

"You took me to Dan Barber's Blue Hill once," I said, referring to one of the chefs on the hit list.

Simon glanced up from the computer screen. "You ordered the Brussels sprouts appetizer, and the horseradish sauce made you sneeze. It was the daintiest sneeze I'd ever heard—a soft little 'tch' instead of a loud 'ha-tschoo.'"

"Sweet of you to remember," I said before refocusing on Ronnie's document. "Well, what do you know? Jason Hill is at the top of his hit list. He probably intends to take out each chef, one by one, in order to restore America to the land of Olive Gardens and Applebee's."

"It's a stretch to imagine someone killing someone over restaurant trends, but if the week here has taught me anything, it's that people take this foodie stuff very seriously." He checked his watch. "We need to shut down both computers and get going."

"Right."

We hurried over to Lake and Gabriel's cottage, which was antiseptic compared to the Gumpers's. Not a stray article of clothing on the floor or errant hair in the bathroom sink. No bags of amaranth. No crossed-out photos of Chef Hill or hit lists on their computers, either. But a document in Lake's sleek white Kate Spade carryon bag caught my attention.

"Simon?" I motioned him over, waving the pages. "Judging by all the 'whereases' and 'heretofores,' it's some sort of legal document that's dated a month ago." I handed it to him.

"Cushman & Wakefield," he said, pointing to the letterhead. "That's where Gabriel works."

"And Planet Empire is Chef Hill's corporation," I said. "We're looking at an agreement between the two companies, right?"

"Yeah, it's a lease," said Simon. He gave it a quick read, then looked up. "And it'll blow your mind."

"Tell me, tell me." I jumped up and down like Crazy Connie.

"Jason Hill has leased space in New Jersey in the Paramus Park Mall," Simon explained, shaking his head in amazement. "He's opening a fast-food restaurant called Burger Mania—your basic McDonald's."

"No."

"It's right here."

"So the farm-to-table king is a sell-out?"

"Let me read the post-it that's attached. It says: "Dear Gabe. I understand you were reluctant to handle this transaction, but I'm glad you did. Paramus Park has been a valued client for many years, and our job is to lease space that'll promote growth for all the businesses in the mall. Our personal opinions about the businesses themselves are of no importance. Please keep that in mind. Remember, too, that this transaction is confidential unless and until Jason Hill's people decide to announce his involvement. Your discretion in this matter is appreciated. That being said, it's rather hypocritical that a chef who personifies clean, healthy eating would be launching a chain of greasy burger joints. I guess he's more interested in making money than saving the planet. Such is life. Regards, Adam.""

I was dumbfounded. Dumbfounded! "So Mr. Purity-in-Food is a fraud, just like the murderer's letter said. For what? To buy more yachts? Or support his coke habit? And why did the Vanderkloot-Arnolds bring the lease to Whitley?"

"They worshipped Chef Hill and his food philosophy,"

Simon said. "Maybe they feel so betrayed that they plan to wave the lease in his face and kill him."

"They sure pretend they still worship him," I said. "But the letter writer boasted about doing just that." I inhaled deeply and recalled the recent and very weird conversations with Lake and Gabriel. "Maybe writing the letter and murdering the chef was the 'life choice' they said they were wrestling with. Incredible, isn't it? We have four suspects already and we're just getting started."

Simon placed the document back in Lake's carryon bag. Then he tapped his watch again. "Got to keep moving, Slim."

Next up was Beatrice's cottage. The first thing I noticed upon entering was her cell phone. It was on the dresser, and I assumed she'd left it there because phones were verboten during our agritourism activities.

"Let's see if Mrs. Birnbaum has any messages," I said, picking up the phone and powering it up. "Yup. She has one. Care to listen?"

Simon put his ear next to the phone. "Ready when you are."

"Mrs. Birnbaum, it's Jason Hill. I got all six thousand of your messages, and in case you didn't notice, I'm a busy guy and couldn't drop everything to call you back. What's your problem anyway, lady? All I did was ask you if your son would be interested in coming to work for me when we met at that charity thing in Palm Beach. For Christ's sake, it was at least two years ago. He was the one who told me he wanted to get into the business. When he showed up here at Whitley, I didn't say anything about meeting him before because you strong-armed me not to. But what's the big deal if he apprentices at the Chicago restaurant? Sure he'd have to start from the ground up—he has no restaurant experience—but it would be a nice spot for a guy who wants to change careers at his age. And if I do offer him a job at the end of the week, it'll be up to him to say yes or no. I mean, he's out of diapers and probably makes his own decisions. So chill out, would you please, and leave me the hell alone."

"And she told me she thought her son was controlling," said Simon. "Your boyfriend's mother is a complete loon-ball."

"Wait, so let me get this straight," I said. "Jason Hill has been thinking of offering Jonathan a job in Chicago—a job that would not only take him away from his father's law firm but leave Beatrice all by herself in Palm Beach? I'm not surprised she's upset. Talk about a possible motive for murder."

"She wouldn't have made a good mother-in-law anyway," said Simon, consoling me with a kiss. "Have I told you I really like you in that apron?"

"Yes." I wriggled out of his embrace. "We have five bona fide suspects now, Simon. Five."

"I'm willing to wager that your boyfriend will make six."

When we let ourselves into Jonathan's cottage, I showed Simon the three cookbooks. "He brought them all the way from Palm Beach. Strange, right?"

Simon flipped through the pages of the first cookbook. "Looks like your boyfriend does have a grudge against the chef—a major-league one."

I gasped when I saw that a recipe in the chapter on vegetables, the one for fried cauliflower, pumpkin seeds, and glögg (whatever that was), had been circled and marked with the word "plagiarized" in bold letters. In the chapter on meats, there was a recipe for pheasant breast, turnips, cranberries, and potato-celeriac pave (whatever that was) that had been similarly circled and marked. "Jonathan is accusing Jason Hill of stealing his recipes?"

"So it seems."

The other two cookbooks contained more recipes that Jonathan had deemed plagiarized. I'd heard through one of my book publishing clients that chefs were often accused of stealing each other's recipes and passing them off as their own, but would an icon like Chef Hill steal recipes from a food blogger, particularly since he disdained bloggers?

"Chef Hill's cookbooks are probably cobbled together by his employees without much quality control or oversight," said Simon. "They could be full of bootlegged content."

"Maybe Jonathan found out he'd been plagiarized after he met Chef Hill two years ago at the Palm Beach function," I theorized.

"And he lugged the cookbooks to Whitley to confront the chef and kill him," said Simon.

"No, I'm not buying it," I said. "He's too levelheaded to commit murder. He bought me flowers and danced me around his cottage and told me I was his destiny."

Simon couldn't resist a smile. "You don't believe in destiny, Slim. You told me that the first time we made love. You also said I was too handsome to take seriously, that you thought guys who looked like me were bound to cheat."

"Must have been a real turn-on. Sorry."

"I forgive you. Want to break into Alex's cottage and call it a day?"

"Sure."

We arrived at Alex Langer's cottage, took a quick inventory of her belongings, and discovered that she was a notetaker. Like every decent hotel, Whitley provided a pad of paper by the phone, and Alex had scribbled all over hers. Her penmanship was terrible, but I was able to make out that she'd written a "To Call" list. At the top was Rick, her fiancé.

"It's kind of odd that she has to remind herself to call him," I said. "Not that I know anything about having a fiancé."

Simon ignored my jab. "She's got other names on here," he said, reading the list over my shoulder: someone named Danny, a Doctor Nash, a spa called Clouds, and Saks, Neiman's, and Bergdorf's."

"Interesting. Alex dresses like a Boho chick, but her taste in department stores is Upper East Side Princess," I said. "Maybe Rick pays for her clothes like he paid for her week at Whitley and her diamond engagement ring, not that I know anything about diamond engagement rings."

"You never quit, do you?"

"Feel free to go back and join the other agritourists if I'm too aggravating," I said. "They're probably still eating chocolate marquise—"

I heard a noise outside the cottage door and froze.

Simon reached for my hand and hustled me into the bathroom just as someone entered the cottage. As he and I hid in the rainfall shower, I prayed that the shower door, which was made of a custom glass etched and sandblasted with designs of farm animals, would obscure us in case Alex came in to pee. I also wondered why Jackie and Pat hadn't kept her busy like they were supposed to.

While Simon looked as calm as a person who hid in

people's bathrooms every day, I remained rigid, frantically thinking of what our reason for being there could be if Alex did indeed find us. I had diarrhea and her cottage was nearby? Simon got sweaty and needed a cold shower? We both had something private we wanted to talk to her about? They were all idiotic reasons, so I gave up and just stood there quaking.

"Hey babe. Miss you."

She must have come back to call her fiancé, I thought, perfectly happy to eavesdrop rather than have to explain our presence.

"Yup, I'll be ready," she said in response to something he'd said. "Oh yeah," she went on. "I've had a great time here. Wait till you see what a good cook I am now." She laughed, then after a beat: "No, babe. He didn't teach us how to make enchiladas or any of your other Mexican favorites." She listened for a few seconds, then: "I know, babe. But it'll be a celebration of us, of what a great team we are. Don't let the details throw you. Let me handle everything."

So they're planning their wedding, I thought. How sweet. I wondered if the event would be held in the city or if it would be one of those overly complicated "destination weddings" where everyone is forced to fly to some remote location they can't afford. I wondered if Rick had a mother like Beatrice whom Alex would have to placate. I wondered if she would quit her hygienist job as soon as she was Missus Whatever-Rick's-Last-Name-Was.

"You sound stressed about it," she said. "I get that it's a big step, but it'll all work out, I promise."

Wow. Rick was one nervous groom. Maybe he wanted Alex to nail down a venue, a caterer, a florist, and a photographer, never mind get invitations out on time, and she'd been too preoccupied with her screenplay to carry out her bridezilla duties. When I'd fantasized about Simon and me getting married, I pictured us doing the deed at my apartment, simply, tastefully, saying our vows in front of one of those celebrants who gets ordained on the Internet, our close friends and family beside us, a harpist plucking little heavenly notes before and after the ceremony. Of course, I now had to erase that particular fantasy from my mind because it wasn't coming true.

"Yeah, it's called Bounty Fest, and they're having pig roasts and hayrides and quilting," said Alex. "Very Americana. Oh and they're having a bunch of country bands playing all day, which you would love. I still can't believe you're a fan of country. It's so not you. Right, right, you should go," Alex said. "I need to get back to my friends anyway." She laughed again. "Yeah, I made friends here. These women call themselves the Three Blonde Mice, would you believe. Picture the types who go to Vegas for girlfriend trips, do shots until they can't see straight, get laid, and act like they don't remember it the next morning."

The nerve! She was making fun of Jackie, Pat, and me, to her fiancé—and after we went out of our way to befriend her! She had pretended to befriend us too, pretending to befriend Jackie most of all. Talk about a mean girl. I was tempted to come charging out of the bathroom, wielding the can of the Bumble and Bumble Full Form Mousse that was in the shower and spraying it right into her eyeballs.

Simon couldn't miss how mad I was. He squeezed my cheeks closed so my lips were immobilized and I couldn't blurt out anything stupid. It didn't keep me from wondering whether being a mean girl meant being a murderer. We didn't find anything that tied her directly to Chef Hill other than that she wanted to interview him for her screenplay, but was she faking that part, too? Did she have another, more sinister reason for wanting to get him alone? I couldn't dismiss her completely as the letter writer, but it was more likely that she was just one of those women who latched onto other women when their men weren't around and dumped them as soon as they were no longer placeholders.

"Okay, bye, babe," she said as I fumed. "Yup, definitely. Love you."

Alex left the cottage within minutes of ending her call to Rick. She did not come into the bathroom. She did not know we were in her shower. She did not know I had just heard her trash Jackie, Pat and me. She wasn't a Boho chick. She was a Boho bitch.

Simon and I waited a reasonable period of time before leaving her cottage. While he went back to the kitchen to join the others, I sprinted to the housekeeping barn to return the keys. Unfortunately I sprinted right into Rebecca, and she did not look happy to see me.

24

"I want all three of you off the premises," Rebecca huffed, flicking her Willie Nelson braids behind her. Jackie and Pat were sitting on little stools in the housekeeping barn, a bare space with nothing but lockers and a wall mirror. They were wearing hangdog expressions, as if they were children just put in time-out by their teacher. I remained standing, defiant.

"Why?" I asked. "Because we caught you and Wes, and you're afraid we'll tell his wife?"

"How I spend my downtime is none of your business," she said. "It's about your behavior, not mine. All three of you."

Rebecca went on a rant about how we'd harassed Chef Hill, harassed the other guests, and harassed her. "You even harassed Sonia, one of our housekeepers," she said, pointing at me. "You're not the sort of people we want at Whitley."

"But you can't kick us out," said Jackie. "We paid for the whole week, and it's only Friday. Checkout is noon on Sunday."

"I can and I am," said Rebecca, her cheeks flushing with anger. She may not have had Willie Nelson's beard and mustache, but she did have the fuzz that plagues women of a certain age. It starts with a single stray hair on the chin, and the next thing you know, you've become a furry animal. "As per our policy of dismissing guests who don't live up to our code of conduct, you will leave Whitley within the hour."

"Please don't make us miss Bounty Fest," Pat pleaded, as if she'd just been told she had to skip Christmas. "We have to be there."

She was right about that. We had to save Chef Hill's life at Bounty Fest, whether he thought we were harassing him or not.

"Look, Rebecca," I said, taking a calmer tone with her, a more conciliatory tone. "We're sorry for causing problems. We'll be paragons of virtue from here on. Just let us stay through the festival tomorrow?"

"No, I meant what I said." She wasn't budging.

I wracked my brain for a way to convince her to let us stay, and then it hit me. "As you may be aware," I began, "one of our group members, Simon Purdys, is the editor of *Away from It All* magazine. If we tell him we've been treated badly, it'll wind up in a very negative article about the resort. You wouldn't want bad PR for Whitley, would you, Rebecca?" I smiled, congratulating myself on what I thought was a brilliant stab at blackmail.

She crossed her arms over her chest and narrowed her eyes at me. "I'm not worried. The publisher of *Away from It All* is my first cousin."

"Larry's your cousin?" Simon's boss didn't look anything like this harpy.

"Yes," she said triumphantly. "On my father's side. Now, if we're finished here, the front desk clerk is expecting you and will have your bills all ready upon checkout. Have a safe trip home."

And off she went, probably to the dairy barn for another round with Wes.

I took a stool, sat next to my friends and stewed silently.

"You tried," said Pat.

"You did," said Jackie. "But are we supposed to just leave Simon with this whole fucking mess?"

"We can't," said Pat. "We have to finish what we started. We have to find a way to stay no matter what."

"Simon," I said, another idea forming.

"What about him?" said Jackie.

"He'll put us up for the night in his cottage," I said. "We'll pack our stuff, check out at the front desk, make Rebecca think we left, and then spend the night at Simon's and be at Bounty Fest tomorrow to make sure Chef Hill doesn't get offed."

"But she'll see us there," said Pat.

"Not with the crowds they're expecting," I said. "We'll blend right in, and she'll never be the wiser."

"Okay, but what are the sleeping arrangements?" asked Jackie. "There's only one bed."

"It'll be tight, but the three of us will fit," I said. "It's a king."

"What about Simon?" Pat asked.

"He loves hammocks," I said. "Luckily, there's one on the front porch. Meanwhile, how come you two didn't keep Alex busy during the chocolate orgy? She showed up at her cottage while Simon and I were there—a very close call."

"I turned around to talk to her, and she was gone," said Jackie.

"Yeah, well thank God she didn't have a full bladder," I said.

"Why? Were you hiding in her bathroom?" asked Pat.

I told them what happened, including Alex's conversation with her fiancé. Jackie was furious when I got to the part about Alex not giving a shit about us.

"Who cares if her fiancé has a nice brother?" she steamed. "I wouldn't want her for a sister-in-law."

"Our hurt feelings aside, I doubt she wrote the letter," I said and gave them a rundown on Connie's *x* on Jason Hill's photo, Ronnie's hit list of chefs, Lake and Gabriel's fast food restaurant lease, Beatrice's voice mail message from the chef, and Jonathan's plagiarism indignities.

"Jason Hill is a douchebag," said Jackie. "Almost everybody seems to want him dead."

"I'm going with Connie," said Pat. "She's the only one who admitted she's mad at him."

"True, but the letter wasn't written in her voice at all," I said. "It just doesn't sound like her. It doesn't sound like Ronnie either."

"I think Lake wrote it," said Jackie. "I'm not as gung ho as she is about this farm-to-table business, but even I'm pissed off that Chef Hill is doing a burger chain. Maybe she and Gabriel are planning to kill him together, or maybe Gabriel won't go along with it. Remember how she said he was too conventional? Maybe she's doing it by herself."

"Or it's Beatrice," I said. "She must be panicked that Chef Hill might steal Jonathan away from her."

"I hate to say it, but Jonathan could have a motive too,"

said Jackie. "If Chef Hill had been lifting my recipes and taking all the credit, I'd go berserk."

"Yeah, but you'd sue him, not kill him, and you'd probably lose," I said. "According to my publishing client, you can't copyright a recipe. You can only copyright the way it's described, as in the text in the cookbook that represents the author's style of expression."

"All the more reason for Jonathan to be pissed," said Jackie. "He's a lawyer, so he knows about the copyright thing. Maybe he tried scaring Chef Hill with the letter, and when he didn't get a response he decided to go ahead with the murder tomorrow."

"Tomorrow." Pat shuddered. "How are we going to stop this from happening when we don't know which one of them is planning to do it?"

We still couldn't come to a consensus about the letter writer, so we went back to our cottages and started packing.

I was stuffing clothes into my suitcase when I realized I hadn't checked my e-mail in hours—too many distractions. There in my inbox was one from Olivia Martindale, my British colleague in Pearson & Strulley's Palm Beach office, the one I'd written to about Jonathan. She apologized for the delay in responding and had this to say about him:

Big-time lawyer. Big-time philanthropist. Big-time player.

Big-time player? Jonathan?

If your interest in him is personal, Elaine, avoid at all costs. First wife, a doctor, caught him in bed with a stripper. Second wife, a realtor, caught him in bed with the neighbor. Incapable of keeping his trousers on. All he cares about is shagging women. Total arse, sorry.

I was standing when I read the e-mail and now I had to sit down to digest it, such was the sinking feeling in the pit of my stomach. So Jonathan was an arse. I mean ass. I hadn't seen that coming, I really hadn't. Olivia's version of his marital infidelities was the opposite of his version in which he'd been the aggrieved party, and I had no reason to doubt her. What a liar he was! What a creep! He and his mommy were both creeps! She probably hounded him about the women he'd married and how they weren't good enough for him, and he probably took out his twisted feelings for her on them. And to think I'd let him touch me! To think I'd considered him boyfriend material! To think I'd contemplated a future with him! Clearly, my judgment about people was as reliable as my cooking skills.

Well, now I had to take a fresh look at Jonathan as a suspect. Maybe Jackie was right and he was our letter writer. He had motive. He had opportunity. And he had a way with words.

I resumed my packing with a vengeance. I couldn't wait to get back to the city, where the murderers acted like murderers.

Day Six:
Saturday, July 20

25

Bounty Fest didn't open until 10:00 a.m., but when Simon, Jackie, Pat, and I got there at 9:30, we had to fight our way onto the grounds. Whitley was already overrun with at least 300 people from the community and beyond—families with small children who'd come for the hayrides and chicken races, Manhattanites with weekend country houses who'd come for seminars in beekeeping and composting, and hungry, curious locals who'd come to sample the farmer's market offerings. I had no idea how we could possibly pick the murderer out of the crowd, let alone from the members of our agritourism group, but we'd have to try.

"Coffee," Jackie groaned. "Someone steer me to the right kiosk so I can wake up."

"Me too," said Pat, as the four of us squeezed past sweaty body after sweaty body to get to the Grind Your Own Coffee Beans stand.

"I didn't get ten minutes of sleep," I complained. "I forgot you both snore."

"I slept like a baby in the hammock," said Simon, the only one of us whose eyes weren't puffy. "I'm up for another sleepover whenever you guys are."

"No thanks," said Jackie, after she'd taken her first sip of her Jackie Gault Natural Vanilla Bean Latte (they gave you a cup with the name of your personal brand on it).

"Once we're fully caffeinated," I said, "I think we should head over to the chef's tent so we'll be on top of things before Chef Hill gets there. According to the activities sheet, he does forty minutes on pickling vegetables, takes a twenty-minute break, comes back for another forty minutes on using farm eggs, then takes another twenty-minute break, and comes back for the final forty minutes on six ways to incorporate Swiss chard into your life."

"Sounds like a plan," said Jackie, who was so sleep deprived that she spilled coffee on her jeans. We all swabbed at her legs with napkins until she was dry.

"Uh-oh," said Pat. "I think I see Rebecca. What if she throws us out?"

"Just keep your head down, everybody," I said. "And move fast."

There were more than 200 people waiting for Chef Hill to show up inside a large tent erected for his demos. Bales of hay had been strategically placed in rows for everybody to sit on. Live country music was playing at an ear-splitting volume from a nearby bandstand, making it difficult for us to hear one another.

"I think we should wait in the back so we can see who comes and goes," I shouted as the four of us surveyed the scene.

Chef Hill entered the tent looking very "hopped up," as

my mother would say. His coke habit had to be pretty bad if he couldn't perform at a simple farm demo without a few pre-show snorts.

"Here comes our cast of suspects," said Simon.

We all turned to look. Lake and Gabriel wore annoyed expressions, as if they were being dragged to the funeral of someone they couldn't stand. Connie and Ronnie didn't seem happy either; her mouth was set in an angry line, and he was glowering as he stuffed his face with a muffin. Beatrice and Jonathan arrived together, but awkwardly; he strode in ahead of her instead of holding her arm as he usually did, and she struggled to catch up to him, her eyes pleading with him not to be left behind.

"I wonder where Alex is?" said Jackie.

No sooner did she utter the name of our fake friend than we saw Alex approaching the entrance to the tent. She was in one of her flowing outfits, bandana and all, and carrying her Whitley tote bag—and she was not alone. She was with a brown man. I don't mean the color of his skin. I mean that he had brown hair, a brown sunhat, a brown Polo shirt, and brown slacks.

"Elaine, isn't that Eric?" Pat said, pointing at Alex and her escort.

I couldn't speak. The closer he got, the more my brain shorted out. It was one thing when Simon showed up at Whitley unexpectedly. That was heart attack worthy enough, but at least he'd come with my friends' blessing, besides which I loved him. But Eric? Eric Zucker? My dreaded ex-husband? The man who alphabetized the prescription drugs in his medicine cabinet and organized the food items in his refrigerator according to their sell-by dates and actually had one of those scented deodorizer trees hanging from the rearview mirror in his car? The man who cheated on me with Lola, makeup artist to the stiffs? *That* Eric? What the hell was he doing with Alex Langer at Bounty Fest?

"Hey, everyone," she greeted us. "Meet my fiancé, Rick Zucker. He took the day off and came up here a day early. Say hi to the Three Blonde Mice, Rick."

Rick? She called Eric *Rick?* All this time when she'd been going on and on about her wonderful, generous, diamond-ring-gifting fiancé, the guy to whom she was always giving blow jobs, she'd meant Eric? He did have a brother who was a lot nicer than he was, but not nearly nice enough to fix up with Jackie.

"Hello, Elaine," he said with the monotone of the undertaker he was. "What an unfortunate coincidence."

"Hello, *Rick*," I said. "So you're finally remarrying. I never thought you'd find a woman willing to put up with you. Are you still lining up the spices in the kitchen by color? I could never figure out which went first among the reds—paprika, cayenne, or chili powder—but I guess Alex is better at it."

"What did you say, Elaine?" Alex shouted. "I missed that. This band is *loud!*"

"Elaine was just reminiscing," Eric told her. "Try not to laugh, sweetie, but she's the ex-wife I'm always talking about—the one that gives me those nightmares when I wake up in a cold sweat."

"This is Eric?" Simon said to me. "Your Eric?"

"He's not my Eric," I said indignantly and pointed at Alex. "He's all hers."

"You're kidding," she said to her fiancé with a stunned giggle. "You and Elaine? Seriously?"

"As serious as cancer," I said. "When's the wedding? You two have been making plans, right?"

"You're misinformed as usual. We haven't even set a date," said Eric.

"We only know we want to be together in the near future." Alex hooked her arm through his and gave it a squeeze.

How odd. When they were on the phone the night before, it sure had sounded like the plans were in motion.

"Are you interested in Chef Hill's farm-to-table cooking?" I asked him, still trying to reconcile what I'd overheard with what they were saying now. "Or did you just come to keep Alex company, *Rick*?" I enjoyed using her name for him. He was so not a Rick.

"I wouldn't know Chef Hill from Jonah Hill," he said. "Food is food to me. Well, except Mexican, as you may remember, Elaine. Can't stand it."

I started to give him a smart-mouthed answer about how I'd blocked out most of the gory details of our marriage, but I did remember that when he and Alex were on the phone she had specifically mentioned enchiladas because he'd asked if Chef Hill had taught her how to cook them. Something didn't add up.

"Are you staying for the whole festival today?" I asked Eric, deciding to test the theory that was taking shape in my head. "If so, you'd better buy some earplugs. You can't stand country music almost as much as you can't stand Mexican food, not even guacamole." I turned to the others and laughed. "Who in their right mind doesn't like guacamole except this guy here?"

"Sure I think country music is boring," he said, "just like bitter ex-wives who dredge up their sad pasts every chance they get."

I ignored his abuse and focused on the three discrepancies in Alex's phone conversation with her fiancé: she seemed to be planning a wedding and now Eric was saying they weren't; she said he loved enchiladas and he said he couldn't stand Mexican food; she said he was a fan of country music and he said it was boring. It didn't take a genius to put three and three together and figure out that the man Alex was talking to, the man she identified as "babe," the man to whom she said "I love you," wasn't Eric Zucker. She was a phony friend to us and she was a phony fiancée to him. The question was why?

I thought back to the other names on her "To Call" list by the phone in her cottage: the department stores and a doctor and a man with a boy-next-door sort of name. Arnie? Frankie? Stevie? No, no, it started with a *d*. Danny. That was it. Had she called this Danny person and told him she loved him while Simon and I hid in her bathroom? Was she having an affair with him even though she was engaged to Eric? Was she leading some kind of double life?

Why would she bother? Was it really Eric's money she was after? Or was he her cover—a shield of legitimacy for when she killed Chef Hill? Yes, Jonathan had vaulted into the number-one slot on my suspects list, but maybe she'd asked Eric to come to Whitley a day early so he could be her unwitting getaway driver. He really was gullible enough not to see through her if she did lead a double life. The question was why would she lead a double life, and what was her possible motive for wanting to kill Jason Hill?

"Why don't we go sit down, sweetie?" Eric suggested to her.

"You're allergic to hay," I reminded him, stalling for time so Alex wouldn't slip away. "You'll have a wheezing attack if you sit on one of those bales."

He gave me a "none of your business" look and said, "I take medication for that now, Elaine."

"Okay, but I haven't formally introduced you to my friends," I said, and did just that. "I met Jackie and Pat the day I divorced you. We went out and celebrated."

My friends nodded, not knowing exactly how to react to the sudden appearance of my ex and the volley of insults between us.

"I celebrated after our divorce, too," he said. "I bought Lola a mink coat."

"Of course you did, since nobody wears fur anymore," I said, rolling my eyes. "And this is Simon, my boyfriend."

Simon smiled. "So we're back to calling me that?"

"Not now," I muttered to him.

"Let's sit down, Rick," said Alex, clutching her tote bag and trying to steer him away. "I really want to watch Chef Hill cook."

"Great! We'll join you!" I said merrily, gesturing at my cohorts to follow them.

There weren't enough bales for all of us to sit together, so our team sat a few rows behind the charming couple.

"I can't believe your ex is here," Jackie said.

"Was he always so grumpy?" said Pat.

"All I can say, Slim, is I'm a big upgrade over that guy," said Simon.

"Could we focus, people?" I asked. "I think Alex wrote the letter, that she's our killer."

"Just because she's manipulating Eric?" said Jackie. "Doesn't make her a killer. We need a motive."

"And we need one fast," said Simon. "If Chef Hill's biting the dust, it'll probably happen during one of his breaks."

"I'm sticking with Jonathan," Jackie said, nodding two rows down. He was sitting next to Mommy, but they weren't speaking, just staring blankly at the stage.

"Lake and Gabriel are fighting," said Pat. "Look at them."

The Vanderkloot-Arnolds, who were three rows down, were engaged in a shouting match all right, but they were drowned out by the music, so we couldn't make out their words. All we knew was that he was gesturing wildly at her, stabbing his finger in her face no matter how many times she batted it away. Was he trying to talk her out of her plan to kill the chef over the burger chain? Was he defending himself against her accusations that he wasn't man enough to help her commit the crime? Or were they arguing over the pregnancy issue and merely having a domestic quarrel?

"Connie and Ronnie aren't fighting, but they're not happy," said Jackie as we all glanced in their direction over to the left. "Remember how crazy excited she was about seeing Chef Hill in the beginning of the week? Look at her now: one big scowl."

"And Ronnie's wearing one of those vests with pockets that conceal weapons," I said. "Pretty suspicious in this heat, right?"

"Not if he filled the pockets with muffins," Simon said.

"Good morning, everybody. Nice turnout today, huh?"

Chef Hill had begun his program, his minions scrambling to set up all the prepped ingredients, the country music band singing and strumming in the background.

"We're kicking off the demo with pickling, the process that preserves our veggies all year long so the farm experience is always with us," he said. "Let's get cooking—bang bang."

He started with beets. He cut them up, boiled them, drained them, rinsed them in cold water, peeled the skins off, sliced them, and plopped them in vinaigrette. "Let them marinate for half an hour at room temperature," he said, "and then eat 'em, store 'em, have 'em by themselves as a side dish, or throw them in with other pickled veggies."

He moved on to cucumbers, cabbage, tomatoes, artichokes, asparagus, and peppers and pickled those, too— or his assistants did, since there were only forty minutes to each session. When he was finished, everybody applauded, and he hopped off the stage for his break, and his crew cleared the demo table and set up for the next show and tell.

I kept an eye on all our suspects throughout the demo to make sure they hadn't budged. They were still accounted for even during the break.

"Mildly interesting about pickling all those vegetables," said Simon. "But if you ask me, Chef Hill was pretty pickled himself."

"You think?" I said.

"Definitely a cokehead," he confirmed. "And all that 'bang bang' stuff has gotten really old."

"It got old on day one," I said. "I was ready to kill him myself by day three."

Eventually, Chef Hill's twenty-minute break was up and he was back onstage at the demo table. I stayed glued to our suspects' every move during the forty minutes of recipes for farm fresh eggs—from spaghetti carbonara to frittata with green lentils and smoked trout.

"He's not a bad cooking teacher," Simon commented as Chef Hill left the stage for his second break. "How he finds time to do this gig with all his other projects I have no idea. Why even bother to have a channel on YouTube with instructional videos when you've got so many restaurants?"

"How did you know he has a whole channel on YouTube?" I said. "The letter only mentioned the video where he talks about pudding."

"First of all, I went on YouTube yesterday and watched the channel," he said. "I was looking for clues. Second of all, Alex told me about it during the cheese making. Or was it the fish day?"

"You cooked with me during the fish day," I reminded him. "We made salmon carpaccio together."

"I loved cooking with you, Slim, even if you did have a heavy hand with that mallet. Maybe we could try again at my place next week. I'll buy some of the stuff we made with the group and we'll take a crack at it ourselves."

"About the videos," I said, my anxiety level rising. "If Alex told you about them, she must be our letter writer."

"Not necessarily. She could have watched them to research her screenplay."

"A hundred bucks says there is no screenplay."

"You're on."

I glanced over at Alex. Eric was still sitting on his bale of hay, but she and her tote bag were gone.

26

Jackie, Pat, Simon and I bolted for the row where Eric was playing RhinoBall on his iPhone.

"Where's Alex?" I asked, trying to catch my breath, which was coming in shallow spurts.

"The ladies room, I guess," he said.

"Then why did she take her tote bag with her?" said Jackie. "She could have left it with you."

"Maybe she wanted to put on some lipstick, comb her hair, spray herself with perfume," he said. "How do I know why you women do anything? I don't even know why she wanted to come to this bounty thing except that she likes the cockamamie chef. She even has a nickname for him."

We all looked at each other as if our lives depended on the nickname, as if Chef Hill's life depended on it.

I put my hand on Eric's shoulder in an effort to show him I came in peace. Touching him was like petting a brown snake. "What's the nickname?"

"Lemme think," he said. We were all in agony waiting for his answer. "Custard. Or maybe it's Jell-O."

"Could it be Pudding?" asked Simon.

Eric snapped his fingers and nodded. "Pudding. Go figure."

Bingo. So Alex must have written the letter. "Listen, Eric," I said. "I hate to break this to you, but your fiancée is about to kill Chef Hill unless we find her right away."

He sighed. "Elaine, you haven't changed. You're still a neurotic shrew. You really need to get over the sour grapes too. I've found someone else. I'm happy with her. Deal with it."

"Hey, don't talk to my girlfriend that way," said Simon.

Eric looked at him with pity. "You have no idea what you're in for."

"Enough, okay? This isn't about me," I said. "Alex isn't the woman you think she is. We have reason to believe she wrote a letter threatening to kill Chef Hill right here at Bounty Fest, right this second for all we know."

He looked at Simon again and laughed. "Good luck with her, pal. You'll need it."

"Useless jerk," I said as Jackie, Pat, Simon, and I ditched my ex-husband and ran up to the stage, where we tried to coax Chef Hill's assistants into telling us where their boss was taking his break. To our great frustration, all they'd say was: "We can't give out that information."

"It's for his own safety," said Jackie to an androgynous-looking millennial dressed in head-to-toe black, a color that worked in the city but was a poor choice for a sweltering day on a farm.

We got the same stock answer, no matter which

member of his entourage we asked: "We can't give out that information."

"Fine. We'll find him ourselves," I said in a huff. You try to do someone a favor, and this is the thanks you get?

"Maybe he's in the main building where we had the Welcome Happy Hour that first night," said Jackie once we were out of the demo tent and in the middle of the festival grounds. We were being pushed and shoved by throngs of Bounty Festers.

"Or maybe there's a green room and that's where he is," Pat volunteered.

"Whenever Bill is booked on GMA he waits with the other celebrities in a little room before going on the air. It's just outside the studio. They serve coffee and donuts there."

I'd been accompanying my PR clients to green rooms for years. "Not a terrible idea. Maybe there's a tent just for the talent."

"Only one way to find out," said Simon.

We ran. We ran through men, women, and children. We ran through a group of wackos in green costumes handing out kale chips. We ran in and out of tents that were hosting everything from a lesson in making jewelry out of wild berries to a lecture on promoting the nutritional value of spelt. We ran into Rebecca, who shouted to everyone within earshot, "Those people are not supposed to be here!"

She started chasing us, her braids flying, which made us run faster.

"Watch where you're going!" yelled a woman in the tent where people were engaged in a walnut oil tasting. Apparently, Pat had bumped into the woman, causing her to knock over a bottle of oil on the display table, which created a domino effect; the one bottle toppled the bottle next to it and it toppled the one next to it, and within seconds the entire row of bottles crashed to the ground. "Now look what you've done!" cried the woman. "We have an oil spill!"

We kept darting in and out of tents until we had lost Rebecca and circled all the way back to the chef's demo tent. Eric was still sitting on his bale of hay waiting for his fiancée to return from the ladies room.

"Hasn't it occurred to you that it's been way more than twenty minutes and the chef should already have started his session on cooking with Swiss chard?" I said to him as I scanned the tent and noticed that Lake and Gabriel, Connie and Ronnie, and Jonathan and Beatrice were gone too. Was it possible that I had jumped to conclusions about Alex? Maybe the fact that she'd watched a YouTube video of Chef Hill talking about pudding meant absolutely nothing and that her nickname for him was just a coincidence. Maybe one of the other AWOL suspects was bashing Chef Hill over the head with a rolling pin right that very minute.

"Yeah, how long does Alex usually spend in the bathroom?" said Jackie.

"I've never timed her," Eric said sarcastically, but he was finally starting to look concerned.

"Eric, there's something wrong here," I said as gently as I could. "We really need to find Chef Hill and we don't know where to look. Someone wants to hurt him, and we don't know who."

"You people spent the week here, not me," he said. "Where does he go when he wants to get away from all of you?"

"His cottage?" Simon suggested.

We raced back out of the tent, this time with Eric tagging along. He was convinced his fiancée had gone to interview the chef during his break and was now in mortal danger, and he demanded that we find her and save her from whichever lunatic agritourist was on the loose. We hightailed it out of the festival grounds and into the area of the property where the cottages were. When we got to Chef Hill's cottage, we all agreed to approach the situation quietly, delicately, so as not to provoke any of them—not Lake, Gabriel, Connie, Ronnie, Jonathan, Beatrice, or Alex—into turning us into that collateral damage mentioned in the letter.

Eric, however, decided to go rogue. He pushed past us and burst inside the front door yelling, "Alex? Are you in here, sweetie? I've come to protect you!"

We followed him in, and she was there all right.... She wasn't in danger. She was the source of the danger. And forget the rolling pin. She was pointing a handgun at the chef with both hands. It was a small gun but it had a long black metal cylinder attached to the end of it—one of those silencers or repressors or whatever they called them in the movies. In any case, the whole contraption looked longer than the pork tenderloin Jonathan had butterflied and stuffed with pesto.

"Why, Alex? Why? Why? Why?" Eric wailed.

Chef Hill, who had flattened himself against the wall, was quivering in terror, and said in a tiny squeak, "Please help me. She's about to pull the trigger on that thing." In front of him was a coffee table on which there were several lines of coke, along with a credit card and a rolled up dollar bill.

"They can't help you," Alex said, turning the gun on

us. "They've insinuated themselves into a private business matter and now they'll have to bite the bullet, so to speak."

I felt the panic rising up in my throat and swallowed hard. So it was Alex all along. If only I'd guessed right sooner. "Would it be okay if I asked what the business matter is?" I said. My hands were in the air as if I'd just been arrested. I wanted to show her I was in complete compliance; that I didn't intend to attack her or flee, only to talk.

"It's about fiscal responsibility," she said cryptically.

"In the political sense?" I asked. I found it hard to believe that Alex would kill Chef Hill over the balanced budget amendment.

"I meant personal responsibility," she said. "When you owe someone money—a lot of money—and you don't pay it, you pay with your life."

"Chef Hill's a wealthy man," said Simon. "Why would he stiff you?"

"He's not so wealthy anymore." She nodded at the coffee table where the cocaine beckoned. "He was our best customer for a long time and then—pfft—no cash all of a sudden. My boss told him we couldn't let him run a tab forever. Business is business, like I said."

"And that business is dealing," I confirmed as I noticed that Simon was starting to inch away from the rest of us, ever so slowly and surreptitiously toward the other end of the room. I was dying to call out to him, to beg him not to try and be a hero, but I knew him, knew he was going to attempt a takedown of Alex and her gun from behind. It was that damn savior complex of his. He'd gotten his face punched in when he'd tried to rescue me on the *Princess Charming* and now he was at it again.

"Only Colombia's best," she said proudly.

"Alex, please tell me this is just dialogue from your screenplay," Eric pleaded. "It's not particularly good dialogue, but you said you're still on your first draft."

She laughed. "There's no screenplay, you dork. And my job working for Dr. Bill Nash D.D.S. was a cover, just like my engagement to you—total bullshit."

"You owe me a hundred bucks," I would have said to Simon if he'd been right beside me instead of hovering perilously close to Alex.

Eric's shoulders sagged as he looked at her, and a lock of his brown hair fell limply across his forehead. "I should have known something was off when you asked me to bring you here for the week. You're as worthless in the kitchen as Elaine."

I let that one slide since we all had a gun pointed at us.

"But I probably could write a screenplay," Alex went on. "I'm a better-than-average writer. I came up with a dynamite death threat note for our chef friend. It was so convincing it even scared me."

"It scared me too," I said. "You put it in my tote bag by mistake."

"Did I?" She looked surprised but laughed it off. "I did a couple of lines of our best stuff before the welcome party and was really fucked up that night. My bad."

"Why did you write it in the first place?" I asked. "You made it sound like you had a personal vendetta against Chef Hill because of his food philosophy, not the drugs and all of that."

"In case you haven't noticed, a lot of people hate the chef," she said, which made him wince. "Danny wanted to drive him crazy wondering which of them hated him enough to kill him, so I kept the letter pretty generic." Another laugh. "Danny's into psychological torture these days."

"Sounds like a lovely guy," I said. "Danny's the boss you spoke to on the phone yesterday? The guy who likes enchiladas?"

"Somebody's been listening to other people's conversations," she taunted. "Rick was right about you, Elaine. You're a pain in the ass."

"And you're a lowlife," said Jackie.

"A wolf in cheap clothing," Pat chimed in. "That's what you are."

I watched Simon out of the corner of my eye. That Alex now had to monitor a full house—not just Chef Hill but also Jackie, Pat, Eric and me—meant she seemed to have lost track of my boyfriend. And yes, he was my boyfriend again. It's not every guy who'll brave a gun-brandishing crackpot for you. "Listen, Alex, why don't you drop your phallic weapon and tell Danny that Chef Hill was busy pickling vegetables and you couldn't get him alone, and we'll all go back to our lives as if none of this ever happened."

"Could I say something?" said Chef Hill.

Alex whipped around to point the gun at him again. "No, Mr. Farm-to-Table. You're not in charge anymore—bang bang."

She was grinning at her use of his catchphrase when Simon, who was at least a foot taller than she was, reached over her shoulders and grabbed the gun. She was a fighter though, and didn't let go. As we all looked on in horror, completely uncertain how their scuffle would turn out, the gun went off, into the ceiling.

Forget silencers, by the way. There was nothing silent about the sound of that first shot.

"Get down!" Simon shouted to us, and we all crouched down except Eric, who belly-flopped onto the floor.

The next shot landed in one of the chairs.

"Stay down!" Simon shouted again while he continued to wrestle with Alex, who had kneed him in the groin. *This Danny person must have taught her more than a little jujitsu,* I thought, wondering how a seemingly normal girl like her ended up as a hit woman, not to mention a drug dealer.

For what felt like an eternity, she and Simon tussled on the floor, which was covered in coarse, bristly sisal. I prayed that he would come away with a little rug burn and nothing worse and that we could all go home in one piece.

The next shot landed in my left thigh. Well, it didn't so much land as graze the area just above my knee, but what I remember most was an excruciating burning sensation and then a remarkable gushing of blood onto the rug, saturating it. I thought for sure I was about to die or at least pass out until I realized I was alert enough to hear Eric scream like a little boy having a tantrum. The bullet—my bullet—had ricocheted and embedded itself into the right buttock of my facedown ex-husband.

Once Simon had seized control of the gun and pinned Alex to the ground with Chef Hill's help, Jackie called 911, and Pat sat on the floor next to me, applying direct pressure to my wound with Whitley's fluffy white towels. She was trying to stop the bleeding and ended up looking like she'd hosed herself down with ketchup.

It was at that point that I started to lose consciousness from the pain, and I was okay with that now that Simon and my friends were out of danger. But I stuck around long enough to hear Alex say to Eric, "Did you really think I would marry a guy who sews his name in his underwear?"

And then it all went black.

Day Seven:
Sunday, July 21

27

I woke up in a private room at Danbury Hospital, which was only a short ambulance ride from Whitley and more sophisticated than you would expect a local country hospital to be. They had over 300 beds, actual doctors, and most importantly, the latest painkillers, of which I took full advantage.

I had one of those morphine pumps hooked up to my IV, and it eased the throbbing in my leg where I'd been sewn up. Yes, I hallucinated from time to time, but I was lucky the bullet didn't break a bone or shred ligaments, tendons, arteries, and whatever else was in there. I had a wound, that was all, and it would heal. So what if the scar eliminated the likelihood that I would ever again wear a pencil skirt? At my age, pencil skirts were about as attractive on my body as a thong.

Jackie and Pat were hovering over me the first time I opened my eyes, and I felt like Dorothy in *The Wizard of Oz,* when she comes to after the tornado and sees the Scarecrow, the Tin Man, and the Cowardly Lion who turn out to be farmhands that work for Auntie Em. Similarly, I couldn't place my friends exactly, because they were out of context in the strange hospital setting and because my thinking was muddled by an opiate. But when I realized that they were two-thirds of the Three Blonde Mice and that they hadn't been shot or otherwise injured in the melee over the gun, I was so happy to see them that I cried. I hardly ever cried, but I guess the combination of the drugs and the near-death experience made me weepy. (Okay, so I was never near death, but I had lost a lot of blood and gone into shock.)

"Will it hurt if we hug you?" said Pat, her arms already outstretched.

"It'll hurt if you don't," I said, and we clung to one another until an aide came to give me a pill.

"What's this one for?" I asked. Her name was Wanda and she wore blue scrubs. I could never figure out who was who in the hospital hierarchy. The surgeons wore scrubs and the nurses wore scrubs and the aides wore scrubs. The only one who wore a white lab coat was my "hospitalist," the guy who said, "You'll be fine," patted the knee near the wound site, making me wince in agony, and left.

"It's your antibiotic," said Wanda. She filled up my water glass from the pink pitcher on my tray. "Drink."

I drank and thanked Wanda and asked her for a turkey on rye with lettuce, tomato, and mayo. In my morphine haze I had momentarily mistaken her for a waitress. She laughed and told my friends to keep their visit short.

"Am I hallucinating or are you glowing, Jackie?" I asked. "I know you're relieved that I'm not dead—that we're all not dead—but you look happier than you've looked for a while."

She smiled. "I got laid."

"What? How?"

"The usual way," she cackled.

"One of the detectives was very handsome," said Pat. "Very courteous too. Jackie was terribly upset at the police station when we were all giving our statements, so he drove her back to her cottage and calmed her down, and I guess one thing led to another."

"He's not involved in the case," said Jackie. "He just happened to be at the station when we got there. He's off duty next weekend, so we're going out Saturday night."

"That's great," I said. "At least somebody came out of this whole mess with something positive to take home. Tell me about the guilty guests who turned out not to be guilty. Did you see any of them before you checked out?"

"I was at the front desk when Jonathan and Beatrice were paying their bill," said Jackie. "He was hitting on the reservations girl, and Beatrice was having a breakdown over it."

"Pig," I said, referring to my erstwhile suitor. "He and his mother deserve each other."

"Connie and Ronnie told me they made plans for their next trip," said Pat. "They're going to Utah."

"Why?" I said. "Is one of her precious Food Network stars doing classes there?"

"They signed up for a week at the *Biggest Loser* resort," she said.

"It's a fat camp with the same weight loss program as the reality show," said Jackie when I looked confused. "They decided to shed pounds."

"Good for them," I said. "Much more constructive than

killing off farm-to-table chefs. What about the Vanderkloot-Arnolds? Or did they end up killing each other?"

"Nope. They're still breathing," said Jackie. "Breathing fire, in fact. Gabriel told me they're filing a lawsuit against Chef Hill for fraud because he claimed to be someone he's not and charged money based on false pretenses. Or something like that."

"And Rebecca thanked us for protecting her artisan in residence," said Pat. "She called us heroes and gave us gift certificates for another week at Whitley."

"Hypocrite. She can keep her lousy free week." I shuddered after a particularly vivid flashback of how the trip had ended. "Did either of you run into Simon today by any chance?"

"Hasn't he been here to see you?" Pat asked.

"Nope. Not once," I said and started crying again. "I wanted to thank him for what he did—he saved my life, all of our lives—but he hasn't shown up. Doesn't he care how I am?"

"Maybe he had to go back to the police station," said Pat. "There were a lot of details to clear up with all the drug charges."

"Plus the weapons charge and, of course, the assaults," said Jackie.

"Assaults, plural?" I said.

"Don't you remember?" she said. "Eric got shot in the ass."

"Right. How's he doing?" I asked.

"He blames you," said Pat. "He told the police that if the bullet hadn't bounced off your leg, it wouldn't have drilled him in the butt."

I shook my head. "That's Eric for you. But what about Simon? I just can't believe he hasn't come to check on me. Maybe I should sue *him* for fraud."

"Okay, ladies. Elaine needs her rest," said my nurse, who was named Megan and looked like Taylor Swift.

"How old are you?" I asked Megan as my friends took their cue and rose from their chairs.

"Old enough," she said, studying my chart on the computer in the corner of my room. Miss Personality she was not.

"Did anyone ever tell you you look like Taylor Swift?" I said.

"No," she said. "They tell me I look like Taylor Schilling from *Orange Is the New Black*."

"That's the one I was thinking of," I said. "It's the morphine. It's making me fuzzy on my celebrity references."

Jackie and Pat hugged me again and said goodbye, and Megan finished checking my vitals and didn't say goodbye, and then I was alone.

Megan was right: I did need my rest. My eyelids felt as heavy as my wounded leg, which was encased in layers of bandages and elevated on two pillows. I sank into a pleasant state somewhere between sleep and many glasses of wine. It occurred to me that I was enjoying the morphine a little too much and that I should avoid becoming a "dope fiend," as my mother would say.

I was lying there suspended in time, eyes closed, head in the clouds, leg in the air, when a voice penetrated.

"Slim? Can you hear me?"

Of course I could hear him. I wasn't deaf, just injured. But I didn't open my eyes or give Simon any indication that I was awake. *Let him worry*, I thought. Let him think I had only minutes to live. Let him think he waited so long to come and see me that he'd missed his opportunity and I was lost to him forever. That was what he deserved for making me believe in him again, making me believe in us again, and then ignoring me. How could an entire night and day go by without a visit from him? Not a phone call or even one of his stupid texts with nothing but emoji symbols in it. Why did he bother to rescue me if he couldn't so much as—

"Slim, it's me. Simon." He spoke gently, tenderly, and kissed my forehead. "I'm sorry I got held up, but you're not an easy person to shop for, you know?"

Shop for? What was he talking about?

"I'd really like you to wake up so I could ask you something," he went on. "Come on. Open your eyes for me, okay?"

Well, I was curious about the shopping thing, but I decided to play the part a little longer. "Is someone there?" I mumbled, the way I assumed a patient emerging from a deep coma would mumble.

"It's Simon, Elaine. Simon Purdys." He sounded almost distraught.

"I'm sorry. Do I know you?" I was laying it on thick, I know, but I couldn't help myself.

"It's Simon," he said again. "If you can hear me, I want you to know that I'm ready. No more 'almost.' No more limbo. No more your place on Tuesday night and my place on Saturday night. When I saw that gun pointed at you yesterday, it was a wakeup call telling me I was an idiot to keep living in the past. So I'm here to commit to you 100 percent, in sickness and in health, for richer or poorer, when times are good and when somebody's trying to murder somebody. I want to marry you, Slim, as soon as you're out of this hospital, if you still want me. That's why it took me so long to get here once the police were done with me. Litchfield, Connecticut doesn't have a Tiffany's on every corner, so I had to drive to Westport and back. Traffic was awful going southbound on Route 7, but it was all worth it, because the ring I bought you is pretty special. I described you to the saleswoman—I didn't know which kind you'd like—and she said to go with the one I have here. Oh, come back to me, would you? Let me put it on your finger and do this right."

I wasn't saying anything at this juncture, not because I was sadistic and heartless and unforgiving but because I was speechless, overcome with the sort of emotions I had spent a lifetime imagining that a bride in love would feel.

"I'd better get the nurse," Simon said and started to leave.

"Oh, no you don't." I opened my eyes, reached out, and grabbed his wrist. "You're not going anywhere."

He smiled and said, before he kissed me, "No, Slim. I'm not."

Author's Note

The dessert featured in Chapter 22, the **Dark Chocolate Marquise with Beet Cremeux, Beet-and-Raspberry Sauce, and Salted Pistachio Croquant**, was created especially for this book by James Arena, pastry chef at Arethusa al tavolo, Connecticut's hottest farm-to-table restaurant and one of my favorite eateries anywhere. Located in the charming Litchfield County town of Bantam and named a 2015 Top 100 Restaurant in America by Open Table, Arethusa al tavolo is owned by George Malkemus and Anthony Yurgaitis, the president and vice president of Manolo Blahnik, who branched out from the high-end stilettos made famous by Carrie in *Sex and the City* when they started a dairy farm business in Litchfield. Dan Magill, the restaurant's executive chef, recently nominated for a James Beard Award for Best Chef: Northeast, incorporates the farm's heavenly milk, butter, cream, and cheese in his menu items along with seasonal products from around the state, as does pastry chef Arena. If you're ever in Connecticut, treat yourself to a truly memorable dining experience there. In the meantime, below is Chef Arena's recipe for the chocolate marquise, so you can enjoy it at home. Chef Arena conceived it as a way to celebrate the earthiness of the beets and the indulgence of the chocolate. "I like dessert and I like making people happy by offering them a great finale to a meal," he said. (Disclaimer: I've swooned over Chef Arena's dessert at the restaurant, but I haven't tried making it. I'm not as hopeless in the kitchen as Elaine is, but I'm close when it comes to desserts. So try it if you're feeling adventurous, and let me know how it goes.)

Thin Chocolate Crust
- 7 oz. Valrhona chocolate (70% "Guanaja")
- 3 oz. pure cocoa butter

Line a small sheet pan with acetate. Melt chocolate and cocoa butter together in a double boiler or in the microwave in 30-second intervals. Spread a thin layer on the acetate and chill in the refrigerator until set. (Chef Arena says he puts the crust in the fridge, and by the time he makes the marquise the crust is set enough.)

Chocolate Marquise
- 15 oz. Valrhona chocolate (61% "Extra Bitter")
- 6 oz. butter
- 6 eggs, separated and at room temperature
- 3 Tbsp. sugar
- Pinch of cream of tartar

Melt the chocolate and butter together in a microwave or double boiler until warm but NOT HOT. Using a standing mixer with a whip attachment, whip egg whites with the cream of tartar until thick (medium peak). Add sugar and continue to whip until stiff. Add the egg yolks to the warm chocolate mixture working quickly. Stir until they are emulsified and the mixture is smooth and glossy. Fold egg whites into the chocolate mixture in 3 parts; the first should be worked until smooth, while the next two additions should be incorporated with a little more care so as not to deflate the whites. Dispense mixture onto the thin chocolate crust. Place in freezer to set.

Beet Cremeux
- 1 quart beet juice, extracted from a juicer, reduced to ½ cup, simmering on low, and reserved for the sauce
- ½ cup mascarpone cheese
- 1 cup heavy cream
- 2 Tbsp. confectioner's sugar

Mix ingredients until thick and set aside.

Beet-and-Raspberry Sauce
- 1 pint fresh raspberries
- Reserved beet juice from cremeux
- ¼ cup sugar

Slowly simmer all ingredients until raspberries are soft, approximately 10-12 minutes. Puree. Strain. Chill.

Salted Pistachio Croquant
- ½ cup pistachio meats
- ⅛ cup sugar
- ¼ tsp. sea salt

Line a sheet tray with parchment. Grind pistachios to a medium-fine texture in a food processor. Transfer nuts to a sauté pan and add sugar. Over medium heat, stir constantly until sugar starts to caramelize and nuts start to toast. Pour onto the parchment-lined sheet tray. Dust with sea salt. Cool. Once cool, break apart into bite-size pieces.

How to plate the dessert
From Chef Arena: "Put the beet-and-raspberry sauce on the plate with some finesse. You can paint it onto the plate with a paintbrush or make designs with it or whatever you like. Then put the marquise down on the sauce. It's a mousse-like cake, so it can be cut into rectangles, squares, even rounds. Next goes the cremeux. I'd do a quenelle or a nice dollop right on top with the pistachios cascading over it all. Enjoy."

Acknowledgments

Researching a novel about cooking and eating delicious, fresh-from-the-farm food wasn't exactly a chore, but the farmers, chefs, and restaurateurs I consulted made it an absolute joy. Thanks to Laurence Hauben whose Market Forays in Santa Barbara, CA, took our group on a guided tour of the fish market and farmers market and then on to her French country home for a lesson in tossing off the perfect lunch. Thanks to Jean Jones and Sherry Swanson at Jones Family Farms in Shelton, CT, for teaching our class how to cook a true farm-to-table dinner. Thanks to the legendary Dan Barber and his team at Blue Hill at Stone Barns in Pocantico Hills, NY, for the ultimate education in sustainable farming. My meal there was a night to remember. Thanks to everyone at the Silo at Hunt Hill Farm in New Milford, CT, for letting me play farm-to-table chef for a day. Thanks to Clint and Kimberly Thorn, who create magic at their Thorncrest Farm in Goshen, CT. Clint showed me how to milk a cow and Kim showed me how to make cheese from the milk, and

I had a blast doing both. And a huge thanks to Dan Magill, executive chef at Arethusa al tavolo in Bantam, CT, one of the best restaurants anywhere, for spending his valuable time explaining the facts of farm-to-table life. Thanks to his pastry chef, James Arena, for creating the chocolate dessert that appears in this book (recipe included). And thanks to the farmers at Arethusa's dairy farm, who introduced me to the most well-groomed cows I'd ever seen, one of whom was getting a pedicure.

Thanks to Lori Frisbie not only for her ingenuity in interior design but for coming up with the title "Farm Fatales" for this book. I ultimately decided to use *Three Blonde Mice*, but I marvel at Lori's creativity.

Thanks to all the remarkably good natured people at Diversion Books, especially my smart editor, Randall Klein, and Diversion's production overseer, Sarah Masterson Hally, for putting up with my constant queries.

Thanks, always and forever, to my friend and literary agent, Ellen Levine, for simply being the best.

And thanks to my husband, Michael Forester, for being my date for all the scrumptious dinners we had while I researched this book. On second thought, he should be thanking me.

Jane Heller is the *New York Times* and *USA Today* bestselling author of over a dozen titles, including hits like *Female Intelligence, Name Dropping,* and *Some Nerve.* She has been translated into several languages around the world, and nine of her novels have been sold to Hollywood for film and television. Also known for her non-fiction titles, *You'd Better Not Die Or I'll Kill You* and *Confessions of a She-Fan,* Heller has been critically adored for over two decades.

CONNECT WITH JANE:
www.janeheller.com
www.facebook.com/JaneHellerBooks
@janeheller1

Keep reading for
an excerpt from

*Princess
Charming*

Prologue

At six o'clock in the morning on a snowless, frigidly cold day in January, a man stood at a pay phone at the corner of Seventy-first Street and Lexington Avenue in Manhattan. He looked to his left, then to his right, and when he was sure he would not be overheard by passersby, he stepped closer to the phone and picked up the receiver.

He listened for a dial tone and nodded with relief when he heard one. He knew how rare it was to find a public phone that worked. That was the irony of the "high-tech" nineties. You could reach out and touch Sharon Stone on the Internet, but you couldn't call your goddamn mother from a pay phone.

The man took a deep breath and punched in the numbers he'd written on a small scrap of paper. He pressed his ear to the phone and waited. After only one ring, someone answered.

"I'm here," said a man who sounded as if he was expecting the call but dreading it. "What is it?"

"You're going to do something for me," said the caller.

The man on the other end of the phone was silent for a moment. "What's the 'something'?"

The caller cupped his hand around the mouthpiece and said in a hoarse whisper, "You're going to kill my ex-wife."

"Kill your ex-wife?" The man was dumbfounded, nonplussed.

"Yeah, why did you think I was calling you at six o'clock in the morning? To hire you to mow my lawn?"

"No, but I didn't think we were talking about a hit here. That's out of the question."

"There's always the alternative," the caller taunted.

The other man was speechless.

"So. Here's the plan," the caller said when there seemed to be no real resistance. "My ex-wife is taking a cruise next month. One of those seven-day trips to the Caribbean with her two girlfriends. The Three Blonde Mice, they call themselves." He smirked as he pondered the nickname. Sure, all three women had blond hair, but the mousy part was debatable. The Three Blond Barracudas would be more accurate. "The name of the ship is the *Princess Charming,*" he continued. "It leaves Miami at five p.m. on Sunday, February tenth and returns there the following Sunday at seven a.m. I want you to take that cruise and kill her before the ship is back in Miami."

"You want me to kill her while she's on the ship?"

"You'll probably have to use a cover with the other passengers," said the caller, ignoring the man's question. "Hand them a line about why you're taking the cruise. But you're a good liar. I ought to know, huh?"

"Look, I—"

"The main thing is, do it and don't get caught," the caller interrupted. "What do you say?"

Say? What could the man say?

"She deserves to be killed," said the caller, as if reading the man's mind. "You'll be performing a public service, believe me. Besides, killing her won't take up *all* your time on that cruise. You'll be in the Caribbean in the middle of winter, the envy of all your friends. You can hang out at the pool, eat as much as you want, do the shows, the casino, the disco scene. It'll be a goddamn *vacation*."

There was another moment of silence while the man contemplated the unfortunate situation in which he found himself; he wasn't exactly flush with options.

"I'll do the job," he said finally. He did hate cold weather and he did need some sun. So he'd have to kill the woman. At least he'd get a tan while he was at it.

Day One:
Sunday, February 10

1

"How are you today, Mrs. Zimmerman?" asked the ticket agent for Sea Swan Cruises as he examined the small packet containing my tickets, passport, and Customs forms. He couldn't have been more than twenty; he looked callow, unripe.

"I'm fine, thank you," I said, mildly irritated that he had referred to me as *Mrs.* Zimmerman. There was nothing in my documents indicating that I was married, nor was I wearing a wedding band, and yet—

Well, he wasn't the first one to make the mistake. If you're a woman of a certain age, it probably hasn't escaped you that men—particularly but not exclusively *young* men—automatically call you "Mrs.," whether you're married or not. It comes with the territory, like receding gums.

"Sorry to keep you waiting, Mrs. Zimmerman," he said as he continued to inspect my papers.

"Take your time. I'm not in any big hurry." I sighed,

wondering what on earth I was doing in the Sea Swan Cruises terminal in the first place.

Actually, I knew full well what I was doing there. I was embarking on a seven-day cruise to the Caribbean aboard the *Princess Charming,* the crown jewel in Sea Swan's line of 75,000-ton "megaships," because my best friends, Jackie Gault and Pat Kovecky, had talked me into it. The three of us had taken a week's vacation together every year since we were all divorced. We'd gotten herbally wrapped at Canyon Ranch and gone white-water rafting on the Colorado River and run with wolves at some New Age place in the Catskills whose name I've completely blocked out. We'd been skiing in Telluride, sunning in Anguilla, shopping in Santa Fe, you name it. The expression "Been there, done that" just about summed it up—except for a cruise. We'd never done *that.* Until Jackie suggested it back in October, while the three of us were discussing our vacation options.

"Well, why not?" she said when I didn't look especially enthusiastic. "Cruises are supposed to be incredibly relaxing."

"Not if you get seasick," I said.

"You won't get seasick, Elaine," Jackie said. "The ships come with stabilizers now. And even if you did get seasick, they'd give you a pill or something. They do everything for you on cruises. You don't have to lift a finger."

In her professional life, Jackie lifted more than her fingers; she lifted pots of geraniums and bags of fertilizer and saplings of various species. She was partners with her ex-husband, Peter, in "J&P Nursery," a landscaping and garden center in Bedford, New York, a tony Manhattan suburb that was all the rage with upwardly mobile corporate executives, Martha Stewart acolytes, and deer. Jackie spent her days knee deep in dirt—pardon me, *soil*—planting flowers and shrubs for newly minted thirtysomethings who had houses the size of Versailles and didn't know a Venus flytrap from a pussy willow. As a result of the hard, physically punishing work she did, she always lobbied for the sort of vacation that involved no labor whatsoever—an environment where *she* would be ministered to.

I turned to Pat. "What do you think? Are you in favor of spending a week on a boat with the Great Unwashed?"

She considered the question. For what seemed like an eternity. Far be it from Pat to act impulsively. She weighed every decision as if it were momentous, irrevocable, her last, which could be painfully frustrating if all you wanted to do was pick a movie or settle on a restaurant.

"Jackie's right," she said finally, nodding her head for emphasis. "Cruises offer their passengers complete spoilage."

Pat was the queen of malapropisms as well as the slowest decision maker on record. In this case, what she'd meant, of course, was that cruises spoiled you. Pampered you.

"They look after your every need," she said. "Diana and her husband take cruises and seem to enjoy themselves very much."

Diana was Pat's younger sister. Her much more socially active younger sister. When they were babies, their parents had labeled Diana "the outgoing one" and Pat "the shy one," and the labels proved self-fulfilling and next to impossible to shed. But Pat's shyness was deceptive; she didn't say much, but she was unwavering in her decisions, once she made them. For example, it had taken her ex-husband, Bill Kovecky, their entire four years of college to convince her to marry him. Yet once she'd agreed, she was his forever.

Through his stint in medical school, his internship, his residency. Through the births of their five children. Through his metamorphosis into Dr. William Kovecky, the God of Gastroenterology. Through his speaking engagements and television appearances and trips to exotic foreign countries to deliver speeches on ileitis. Through his self-absorption and withdrawal from his family. Even through the divorce. Pat remained loyal to Bill through it all, was still deeply in love with him. She may have been "the shy one," but she had a steely determination, and one of the things she was determined about was winning Bill back. Jackie and I shrugged whenever the subject came up. We weren't exactly experts on winning back ex-husbands, since neither of us wanted ours back. Besides, Bill hadn't married anybody else in six years, so maybe Pat wasn't in total denial. "Yes," she said again. "I think a cruise is a fine idea. Just what the doctor ordered." Since Bill was a doctor, she liked dragging the word "doctor" into as many conversations as possible.

"A cruise?" I groaned. "I really don't think I'm the type, you two." I had nothing against being pampered or spoiled or ministered to. I just didn't want the ministering to take place on an oceanic vessel from which I couldn't escape, should I not be enjoying myself.

"Not the type? What type?" Jackie protested. "From what I've read, there really is no stereotype when it comes to the passengers. Cruises attract a broad cross-section of people."

"'Broad' is the operative word," I said. "You take a cruise and you're stuck on a floating cafeteria for seven days. The food they throw away could feed a small country."

"All right, let me put it another way," said Jackie, in her

husky, ex-smoker's voice. "I haven't gotten laid since George Bush was President. I would like to end the drought before one of George Bush's *sons* is President. Now, I happen to know that single men take cruises. I would, therefore, like to take a cruise. Am I making myself clear?"

"Crystal," I said. Jackie was so earthy. "But you're forgetting something. The single men who take cruises wear jewelry."

"There you go again with your stereotyping," she said.

"And black socks with brown sandals," I said.

"Elaine," she sighed, rolling her eyes.

"And they look like Rodney Dangerfield," I added for good measure.

"Perfect. I could use a good laugh when I'm having sex for the first time in years. I've probably forgotten how to do it," said Jackie. "Look, I think we'd have a great time if we took a cruise, I really do."

"According to Diana, there's a lot to do on a ship," Pat stated, then launched into a laundry list of the activities they offered on cruises. "You wouldn't be bored, Elaine. I'm quite sure of it."

The debate had lumbered on for another hour or so. Jackie and Pat insisted we'd have the time of our lives and I anticipated everything that could go wrong the minute we left dry land. I was a creative, imaginative thinker, which came in handy in my career as a public relations executive but wreaked havoc with my emotional life. You see, my creative, imaginative thinking all too often took the form of what my ex-husband, Eric, used to call my "bogeyman obsession"—incessant forebodings of disaster. What Eric didn't realize was that I was right to be obsessed by the bogeyman because *he* turned out to be one. But more on that later.

In the end, I'd been outnumbered. I'd come to the conclusion that the only way to shut my dear friends up about taking a cruise—they were dangerously close to sounding like a Kathie Lee Gifford commercial—was to say I'd take one.

"It'll be a kick, lying around the pool, not a care in the world, having handsome young studs fetch us piña coladas," Jackie said.

"I suppose I could catch up on my reading," I said, caving in. "And I could jog around the ship's Promenade Deck every morning—unless, of course, the guard rails aren't high or sturdy enough and I fall overboard."

"Oh, Elaine. Get real," she said. "Nothing's going to happen to you on the cruise. It'll be fun. Something different for us."

"Yes, something different," Pat agreed.

How different, they had no idea.

So there I was in Miami that Sunday afternoon in February, standing at the ticket counter inside the Sea Swan Cruises terminal. The *Princess Charming* wasn't shoving off until five o'clock, but our nonstop Delta flight from LaGuardia and shuttle bus ride from Miami International Airport had deposited us at the Sea Swan terminal at twelve thirty.

"My God. Would you look at that," I'd said when we stepped out of the van and caught our first glimpse of the ship. The brochure had said she was fourteen stories high and nearly three football fields long, but nothing had prepared me for the sight of her as she rose out of the water like a

Ritz Carlton with an outboard. The thing was spectacular looking, its white facade and Windexed portholes glistening in the afternoon sun.

"It's majestic," Pat whispered, gazing up at the ship with genuine awe. "And so state of the artist."

After spending a few more minutes gawking at the *Princess Charming,* we'd gone inside the terminal, walked through the same kind of security x-ray machine they have at airports, taken our place on line, and waited. And waited. Ordinarily, I like arriving early for things. When you arrive early, there's no chance of missing the boat, so to speak. But now that I had finally advanced from the line to the ticket counter and was *still* waiting while the agent examined every comma on my Customs form, I was growing restless, grouchy, grim. There was nothing to do but stare at the 2,500 people with whom I would be trapped for a week, searching their faces as they stood in line, wondering which of them—if any—I would befriend over the course of the trip. They came in all shapes and sizes, colors and creeds, ages and affects, the only common denominator being that the vast majority of them were wearing polyester warm-up suits. I wondered what they were warming up for, and then I remembered the ship's fabled midnight buffets and guessed they were warming up for those.

I checked my watch as the ticket agent continued to pore over my documents. I was itching to ship out, get under way, get the whole business over with. Truthfully, I was already thinking ahead to the vacation we would take the following year, the destination *I* would suggest. A theater trip to London, perhaps. Or a week in Key West. Or maybe a trek through Costa Rica. Yes, that was it. Costa Rica. Everyone was going there now. It was a country that was said to be so…so…*real.*

I closed my eyes and pictured myself on the patio of some rustic yet terribly posh Costa Rican inn, mingling with sophisticated foreigners, trading smart little anecdotes, exploring—

"Next!" the ticket agent called out, bringing my reverie to an abrupt end. He handed me back my papers and motioned for Jackie, who was next in line, to approach the counter.

"Good afternoon, Mrs. Gault," he greeted her after glancing at her passport.

"The name's Jackie," she said. I couldn't tell by her tone if she was scolding him for the "Mrs." bit or trying to pick him up.

After what seemed like a lifetime, she, too, was checked in and then Pat took her turn. And while things were at yet another standstill, *I* stood still and observed my friends, shaking my head at the illogicalness of our friendship, at what an unlikely threesome we made.

We had met on the day of our respective divorces, a rainy morning in March of '91 in a sterile Manhattan courthouse. I don't remember who made the first move, but I do remember that Pat was sobbing, that at some point both Jackie and I were consoling her, and that once we determined that we had each come to court to Dump the Husband, we bonded instantly. We sat through all three hearings together, offered each other words of encouragement, and completely ignored our attorneys, who were getting their $250 an hour for showing up at the courthouse so what did they care? By the time the three divorces were final, we had shared intimate details of our marriages, wept, hugged, and vowed to be friends forever.

"The Three Blonde Mice," I had dubbed us that day, and the nickname had stuck.

We three did, indeed, have blond hair—mine, shoulder-length, blow-dried, and streaked; Jackie's very short and utilitarian and strawberry; Pat's wild and frizzy and wheat-colored. And we were about the same age—a year or two on either side of forty-five.

But there were more differences between us than there were similarities, starting with our sizes. I was extremely tall and thin, Pat was squat and chunky, and Jackie was somewhere in between. Consequently, we could never walk in lockstep and were always bumping into each other and mumbling "Sorry." Then, there were the differences in our attitudes toward men. Jackie was always lusting after them, Pat was always comparing them to her God-almighty ex-husband, and I was always wondering how I'd been deluded enough to marry one at all. And then, there were the differences in our personalities and life experiences.

I, for example, was the quintessential neurotic New York City career woman. More specifically, I was an account executive at Pearson & Strulley, the international public relations firm, and except for my annual vacations with Jackie and Pat and my regular visits to New Rochelle to see my mother, my job was my life. I was deeply devoted to burnishing the images of my clients, which included a chain of cappuccino bars, a manufacturer of novelty sunglasses, and an over-the-hill movie actress with an unfortunate habit of breaking the law. I lived in an antiseptically clean, one-bedroom Upper East Side apartment that was guarded by three Medeco locks, two dead bolts, and a lobby filled with a battalion of doormen. I ran four miles a day, rarely allowed high-cholesterol foods to pass my lips, never ventured out in the sun without at least a No. 15 screen, and fearing I might sprout a dowager's hump in my advancing years, had recently tripled my calcium intake. I was a careful, watchful person—a control freak, my ex-husband used to call me—and the aspect of life about which I was most careful was romance. I shunned it the same way I shunned mayonnaise. In other words, if I wasn't working late at the office, I was home alone at night, picking at a Healthy Choice entree and then watching one of those interchangeable magazine shows like "Dateline." *Date*line. Who wanted a date? Not me, no sir. Not after the two most important men in my life had proven to be lying, cheating sons of bitches. I was twelve when I found out about the little popsy my father, Fred Zimmerman, was putting away. Fred had a lot of little popsies, it turned out, and one of them, a redhead with large eyes and large breasts, was so diverting that he left my mother and me for her. Needless to say, I haven't seen his traitorous ass since. My mother got on with her life, marrying Mr. Schecter, our next-door neighbor, a scant seven months after Fred's defection. I, however, was left not only with a desperate fear of abandonment but with a very sizable chip on my shoulder when it came to men. I vowed that I would never be suckered in by a man, never buy into the whole love-and-romance bullshit, never even read mushy novels or sing along with overwrought ballads. When I was thirty-six, I broke two of those pledges. In a moment of abject weakness, I not only went out and bought a Michael Bolton tape; I decided to marry Eric Zucker, who was thirty-eight and, like me, had never taken the plunge. I wasn't in love with Eric, but he seemed like a reasonable antidote to my loneliness and a fairly decent catch, all things considered. His family owned several funeral homes in the Tri-State Area, which meant that he was in a business that would never become obsolete and would relieve me of the unpleasantness of ever having to go funeral home shopping, when the need arose. Eric was nice looking in a brown sort of way—brown hair, brown eyes, brown suits—and he was even more compulsively organized than I was. He actually alphabetized the prescription drugs in his medicine cabinet! What's more, he had the same initials as I did—E.Z.—so there was no need to invest in a new set of monogrammed anything. Best of all, Eric was as uninterested in mawkish emotions and overheated sex as I was—or so I thought. Six months into the marriage, he had an affair with the improbably named Lola, the makeup artist who applied lipstick, eye shadow, and blusher to the embalmed corpses at the family's funeral parlors. I wanted to kill Eric, but I was not a violent person. My lawyer wanted me to take Eric to the cleaners, but I was not a greedy person. My mother wanted me to sully Eric's reputation in the press, but I was not a stupid person. "You're in public relations," she said. "You know how to plant stories about people. Don't take him to the cleaners; just air his dirty laundry in all the gossip columns." I explained to my mother that since Eric was not a celebrity of even minor consequence, the gossip columns would not be receptive to an item about him or Lola. No, I decided to pay Eric Zucker back *my* way. His company's most feared competitor was another chain in the area called Copley's Funeral Homes. So I went after Copley's business with a vengeance, and after two months of groveling, I convinced them to let Pearson & Strulley handle their PR account. I got such positive media coverage for Copley's Funeral Homes that Zucker Funeral Homes lost visibility and customers. A lot of customers. They lost so many customers that poor Lola had to be downsized. "You ruined me and my family, you bitch!" Eric shouted at me during his most recent, verbally abusive phone call. "That's what you get for exchanging bodily fluids with Lola," I said sweetly, hoping Eric would feel at least *some* remorse for what he had done to me.

While I was positively undone by Eric's betrayal when I first found out about it, Jackie acted remarkably nonchalant when she learned that Peter wanted out of their marriage. After their divorce, it was strictly business as usual between them; she never missed a day at the nursery, went right on working side by side with Peter as if nothing had happened, didn't even flinch when his new wife, Trish, who taught first grade at the elementary school around the corner, stopped in to pick up precious little flowering plants for her centerpieces. But Jackie was one tough cookie. She and Peter had started the business right after they were married, and she wasn't about to bow out *or* buy him out, just because he had suddenly decided he was more attracted to a woman who had polish on her fingernails than dirt underneath them. Peter had liked the tomboy in Jackie once, the short, pixie haircut, the athletic body, the salty language, the hoarse, whiskey voice. But as the years went by, his taste changed, and one day he announced that she just didn't "do it for him, sexually." Personally, I thought Peter's rejection of her as a woman was the reason behind her constant chatter about sex—the reason she flirted and undulated and talked about wanting to get laid. It was all talk, as she, herself, admitted, but it was her way of showing the world she *was* sexy, no matter what Peter thought. We all have our shtiks, so who was I to judge? *She* came on to men to ease her hurt; *I* avoided men to ease mine. Jackie was Jackie, and I'd never met a woman like her. She could shoot pool, throw back shots of tequila like one of the boys, and of course, transform people's backyards into pieces of paradise. Ironically, the latest wedge between her and Peter was the very thing that had once bonded them: the nursery. Peter had recently revealed that he wanted to expand the business and sell not only trees and shrubs and landscaping services but vegetables and produce and dairy items. "So you want to turn J&P's into A&P's, is that it?" Jackie had said sarcastically. She was an expert in rhododendron, not goat cheese. There were plenty of places where the yuppies of Bedford could purchase their baby eggplant. What's more, J&P's was doing fine as a nursery. Why tamper with success? Nevertheless, Peter kept telling Jackie that she was holding him back professionally by not going along with his plans. He begged her to let him buy her out of the business, and she told him to go fuck himself. Currently, they were not speaking, except when it was absolutely necessary.

Rounding out our little trio was Pat, the roundest of the three of us. A full-time and very devoted mother, she and her five children and their aging cocker spaniel lived in a rambling white colonial in Weston, Connecticut—a homey, cheerful place where I spent occasional weekends in the summer. I would go to visit Pat, of course, and to get away from the fetidness of the city in August, but a major attraction of the Kovecky household was Lucy, the youngest of Pat's brood and the only girl. She was a nine-year-old with Pat's chubbiness and quiet demeanor, and I, who was not the least bit sticky or sentimental where children were concerned, was mad about her, doted on her, felt a powerful kinship with her. After all, I understood what it was like to have your daddy leave you. Oh, the other kids were nice, too. For males. It was a revelation to me how, in this age of children murdering their parents or, at the very least, toting guns to school, the Kovecky children managed to be good kids who were not nerds. Especially since they were products of divorce. Perhaps it was because Pat never uttered an unkind word about their father, never poisoned them against Bill. And it wasn't as if the children were left destitute. Bill may have turned into a big-shot gastroenterologist who spent more time palpating strangers' abdomens than he did helping Pat with the dishes, but he wasn't one of those deadbeat dads. No way. He made Pat a very generous divorce settlement, and grumble though he did to anyone who would listen, he never missed a payment, even though it meant scaling back his own lifestyle. The reason he and Pat didn't work out was that, somewhere between his first appearance on "Good Morning, America" and the birth of his third child, he decided he wasn't a mere doctor but a healer, a scientist, a saver of the world's collective digestive system. The other problem was that Pat was too shy, too constrained, too afraid of offending him to tell him he was being an asshole. Even her clothes were intended not to offend or call attention to themselves. She wore lacy, frilly dresses that made her look like an English milkmaid in one of those Merchant Ivory movies. She was so shy and self-effacing that her idea of a four-letter word was "oops." She had no self-confidence—at least, until recently. As part of her campaign to win Bill back, she had started seeing a therapist and was adding words such as "empowerment," "needs," and "me" to her vocabulary. She could be a little sanctimonious at times, and I often gave myself a laugh by picturing her locked in a room with Howard Stern, but I adored her. Everyone did. Except Bill, I guess. Although, according to Pat, he had telephoned her just the week before, saying he wanted to see her when she got back from the cruise. Jackie and I prayed it was because he had come to his senses and realized what a decent, loving person she was, not that he wanted to tell her he was cutting back her alimony and child support.

So there the three of us were, bosom buddies in spite of our differences. Three-women friendships can be tough to sustain, given that two are bound to talk behind the third's back and the third inevitably feels left out. But Jackie, Pat, and I were a team, a triumvirate, the Three Blonde Mice. Nothing could come between us.

Of course, we'd never been cooped up on a boat together for seven days.

"All set?" I asked when the Sea Swan ticket agent had returned Pat's documents to her.

"All set," she nodded.

"Then it's show time," Jackie declared.

"We're sure we want to do this?" I asked, still feeling curmudgeonly about the cruise. I really would have preferred that Costa Rican inn.

"We're sure," said Jackie, taking me by the shoulders and literally pointing me in the direction of the sign at the other end of the terminal that read "To the Ship."

We were walking toward the sign when I suddenly decided to call my answering machine one last time. Yes, it was a Sunday, but public relations disasters could and did happen on Sundays. There was always the chance that one of my clients needed me, that Pearson & Strulley needed me, and that I would be duty bound to heed the call.

We stopped at a bank of phone booths. I called my answering machine. There were no messages, but I tried not to take it personally.

As I emerged from the phone booth to join my friends, the man who'd been using the phone next to mine finished his call and spoke to us.

"Hey! Are you ladies sailing on the *Princess Charming* today?" he said in a loud voice, made even louder by the echo-chamber-like acoustics in the terminal.

"Yeah, how about you?" asked Jackie.

"Sure am," he said, then introduced himself as Henry Prichard of Altoona, Pennsylvania. He was in his late thirties or early forties, I guessed, but once men hit middle age these days, there's no way to tell how old they really are. So many of them are having cosmetic work done now—face lifts, collagen injections, chemical peels, you name it. For another thing, they don't permit themselves to look bald anymore, what with plugs and weaves and baseball caps that cover a multitude of sins. This man wore a Pittsburgh Pirates cap, along with tan shorts, a denim work shirt, and penny loafers. He had a hefty, beefy build and ruddy, chipmunk cheeks. I deduced, from the baseball cap, plus the golf bag and the diving equipment, that he was the athletic type. Jackie liked athletic types. "I won the cruise in the company contest.

Best numbers in my district," he added, clearly proud of his achievement.

"You're a salesman?" Jackie asked, as she ran her eyes over him, no doubt assessing his potential in the sex object department. God, this is going to be a long cruise, I thought, worried that Jackie might actually sleep with a man on this trip and that, once her notorious dry spell was over, she'd have nothing else to live for.

"Yup. I'm with Peterson Chevrolet," said Henry.

"Was your prize a trip for two?" Jackie asked, cutting right to the chase.

"Oh, sure. They would've let me take my wife. If I *had* a wife." Henry scoffed at the very notion. "But what kind of woman would put up with a jock? A die-hard Pirates fan like me, huh?"

I looked at Jackie, expecting her to raise her hand, as she was quite a Pirates fan herself, having been born in Pittsburgh. She loved sports, especially baseball, and knew things like batting averages and on-base percentages and which players chewed tobacco and which went for the sunflower seeds. But she restrained herself and said instead, "You must have been in mourning when the Pirates traded Bonds and Bonilla. I know I was."

Henry Prichard's eyes widened and he gazed at Jackie with an almost shimmering respect.

"I *was* in mourning," he said. "But I'm looking ahead to this season. We've got a lot of young kids coming up from the minors, and I'm pretty optimistic about the future."

"Me too," said Jackie, and I could tell she wasn't just talking about the fate of the Pirates. "By the way, I'm Jackie Gault," she said and shook hands with him. Then, almost as an afterthought, she told him Pat's name and mine and explained that we were taking our first cruise.

"Same here," he said. "Which floor are you ladies on? I mean, which deck?"

"Deck 8," Jackie blurted out before I could stop her. Henry Prichard seemed harmless, but you never could tell with people, especially men, many of whom seemed harmless until they landed on the six o'clock news," in handcuffs.

"Aw, that's a darn shame," he said. "I'm on Deck 7."

"Well, maybe we'll run into each other at dinner," Jackie said hopefully. "Which seating did you get?"

Henry checked his ticket, then said, "The one that starts at six-thirty. How about you?"

"We got the six-thirty too," I sighed. I'd been crushed when the tickets had arrived in the mail and I saw that we'd been assigned the unspeakable Early Bird Special instead of the more civilized eight-thirty seating our travel agent had assured us she'd arrange. Now we were certain to be stuck at a table with either octogenarians or howling children.

We chatted with Henry for a few more minutes—I had to admit, he was an affable fellow and I could easily see why he had sold the most Chevrolets in his district—but at some point he cut the conversation short.

"Gosh, I sure can get to talking once I start, but I really do need to make another phone call," he said with a touching, gosh-shucks-heck provincialism about him that people from Manhattan simply don't have. "Why don't you all go on ahead and I'll catch up to you later?"

"Great," said Jackie. "We'll look for you on board."

"Oh, I'll find *you*," he smiled. "Don't you worry."

While Henry and Jackie gave each other a final and

rather provocative once-over, I stole a glance at Pat, who was staring primly at her shoes.

Henry went back to the phone booth, while the three of us turned in the opposite direction.

"He doesn't look a thing like Rodney Dangerfield," Jackie said, elbowing me in the ribs.

"Congratulations," I said. "I hope you two will be very happy together."

"Actually, he looks very much like a cousin of Bill's," said Pat with complete seriousness.

"The hell with Bill," Jackie announced. "The hell with all our exes. Once we're on that ship, they can't touch us."

She cast one more glance back at Henry, who was deep in conversation with the person on the other end of the phone. Then she linked her arms through Pat's and mine.

"Let's cruise," she said, and together we headed for the gangway.

Princess Charming
is available now!